CONTENTS

Editor: Gavin Chappell.

Editorial Assistant: David B Harrington.

Cover art: The Haunter of the Dark by Jarkko Naas

Cover image licensed under the Creative Commons Attribution-Share Alike 3.0 Unported license.

Interior illustrations © 2019 by Dean Wirth.

Lovecraftiana—Vol 4, Issue 1, Walpurgisnacht 2019. Editor: Gavin Chappell. Published by Rogue Planet Press, an imprint of Horrified Press. (www.horrifiedpress.com/)

Lovecraftiana is a quarterly publication dedicated to stories, poems and illustrations inspired by the works of HP Lovecraft. Issues are published April 30, July 31, October 31, and January 31. Copyright © Gavin Chappell 2019. All stories, artwork and articles contained herein are copyright © to the authors and artists credited.

Cover image: xxx

Graphic design © 2019 Gavin Chappell.

Lovecraftiana and its editor accept no liability for views expressed or statements made by contributors to the magazine. This magazine (or any portion of it) may not be copied or reproduced, in whole or in part, by any means, electronic, mechanical or otherwise, without written permission from the publisher, except by a reviewer who may quote brief passages in a review.

Submissions of stories, articles, poetry or artwork on Cthulhu Mythos / Lovecraftian themes can be sent to rogueplanetpress@yahoo.com

ENTOMBED FOR THE CRIME OF INVOCATION by John M McCormick

I can hear them. Their picks and shovels remove the sand that flows around the stone doorway to my tomb. I have been here so long, entombed beneath the swirling sands and kept in utter darkness. I pray they cannot read the warnings on the stone door, or the litany of cursed spells that line the walls leading to my sarcophagus. So much time has elapsed since they entombed me here. Long millennia have passed me by as I have kept faith here in this wretched prison, faith that my forbidden words would find the ear of those who it was forbidden to name. I await freedom from the unescapable darkness, unable even to read the enchantments that adorn the coffin's lid resting just above my face.

I was a peasant in my day, unable to afford the flax linens necessary for the preservation of my corpse. My life was difficult but there was a sweetness to it, and I did not desire my spirit to be lost to the air as my body decayed. There was no benefactor to wrap me in linens upon my death. There were no wise scribes willing to write my name in the eternity of stone, or preserve for me the spells of the dead on valuable papyrus. I was destined to leave this world and face Osiris and Ammit unprepared, the feathers of Ma'at weighing nothing compared to the sins of my heart. I would die ignorant of the spells necessary to navigate the underworld.

Ah, I can hear them, closer still. The sound of chisel and hammer clang rhythmically, reminding me of a time long ago when I shared the freedom of the sun and worked the quarries at the pharaoh's behest. I wonder who these visitors must be, after all this time. Who would encroach upon the vastness of the desert, and wake me from my aeonian slumber? Has the great kingdom fallen? Do the waters blessed by ancient Sebek still flow through the lushness of civilization? I have waited so long here in the confines of blackness to hear those waters flow once more, and taste their sweetness in my withered mouth. I can hear the muffled sound of stone as it falls upon beds of sand, and can hear voices cry out excitedly in a tongue I do not speak nor comprehend. Strangers, then, have found my place of restless captivity. Their work continues, and I wait.

I recall the night they took me. I gathered with others, peasants and noblemen, to worship those whose names we were forbidden to call, and whose images were not to be committed to stone; forces so ancient that they were said to have visited this land and witnessed the genesis of life in the days before man. They were forces of incalculable power, Outer Ones and Elder Gods that had given up this world to a cold indifference aeons before when the gods of Egypt were birthed. We hoped to call their gaze back to us, to be worthy of serving them when our own gods could not meet our needs or our desires.

I feared not the repercussions of my actions, as I had no guarantee of preservation in the afterlife of my nation's chosen gods. I yearned for a continuance of my existence in death, and pled with the forbidden ones for the chance to serve them in immortality. I thought that if, in my poverty, I could not assure a means to enter the blessed underworld at the feet of Osiris then perhaps I could earn my way to immortality through works and devotion to those whose names were hidden from collective memory. And so I found myself bathed in the moonlight, marking yet another high holiday for eldritch gods whose names were known only to a few, and who were spoken of with fearful reverence by reclusive scholars and spat in the baleful whispers of condemnation by other gods' high priests.

Footsteps, now. They approach. The door is wholly breached, I can hear them. Their voices chatter, their footfalls slide along the dust that had settled on the stone ramp descending the short distance to this accursed chamber. Every inch of every stone is covered with curses and evocations meant to warn away grave robbers or other trespassers. There is nothing here to steal. No gold or precious gifts were left here in this tomb, only my corpse. They halt and talk, their alien babbling no doubt centred on the hieroglyphics of the walls, floor, and ceiling. They approach and my body begins to stir after all this time. Their presence has awoken something in me, or perhaps it is something else? A cold sense of urgency takes over. I shift and rattle, my body answering my calls for the first time in many ages.

I recall how the pharaoh's men came that night, so long ago, and the practitioners of forbidden magick all fled. The body was still warm on the altar, the knife blade still dripping with her blood. It looked black in the moonlight. The chants still echoed in my mind as even the high priest dropped his knife and took to the desert:

"Gatekeeper! Hear us! Key-holder! Hear us! Yog-Sothoth is the gate! Yog-Sothoth is the key and Guardian of the gate!"

Perhaps that is why I did not flee with the rest. I focused on the chants, and continued even as the ritual knife clanged against the stone altar. I called out the forbidden name even as the pharaoh's men encircled me. I chanted wildly, transfixed, even as their spears found my flesh.

They took my corpse to the priests, who were fearful of my offending spirit being freed from my corpse and allowed to enter the hidden gate, a gate that once opened may not fully close. They gave me as the fruits of my blasphemy what I never would have achieved in service to their gods, and carefully preserved my body. They removed my organs and placed them in elaborately decorated canopic jars. They wrapped me in fine linens, and coated them in resin. All this time I watched, unable to move, unable to intercede on my own behalf, as the priests initiated death rituals usually reserved for the wealthiest dwellers of my beloved kingdom. All of this they did for a peasant, not out of love, but out of fear. They conducted the ritual for the opening of the mouth, but it was a corrupted ritual with vengeful incantations meant to keep my soul alive in my body while robbing me of my ability to speak my Master's name.

After many days they placed my corpse in a coffin. I could not read the inscriptions, but I heard them recite the curses and describe the sigils painted on the wood. They then placed me in a stone sarcophagus, its face left blank of human features, but inscribed with terrible wards meant to strike fear into the heart of any being unlucky enough to stumble upon it. They sealed the door to my tomb, and though muffled I could make out the reading of further curses, and hear the workman's tools as sigils and wards were inscribed in a final act of disdain against a man whose greatest sin was a desire to find happiness in the next life. Thus I had been entombed for the crime of invocation, robbed of my voice, and labelled a heretic.

These visitors, though, are not afraid. If they can read the inscriptions and incantations they hold no fear of them. I can hear the stone lid to my sarcophagus slide away; the roughness of the sound is pleasantly soothing. Tools bite into the crevice between the coffin's wooden lid and the sides it rests on. For the first time in many years I can see light. Light from their torches. They gasp as the lid is cast aside, their words incomprehensible and suddenly nervous. I stir, the resin of my linen wraps cracking while fabric decrepit with time pulls asunder. I lift my right arm and slowly raise it from the confines of my coffin. I cannot speak, but I point to the ceiling of the tomb as it shatters and crumbles, revealing a blinding light. Their intrusion has upset the delicate magick that hid me from my master's gaze. I cannot speak, but if I could I would shout over their exaltations of terror and tell them that salvation is at hand, for the gate is open, finally, and the Gatekeeper is here.

THE END

ABOUT THE AUTHOR

John M. McCormick is a high school history teacher and college pro-fessor based in southern West Vir-ginia, where he lives with his wife and four children. McCormick was in-troduced to Lovecraft by a student early in his teaching career, and hasn't been able to get the mythos out of his head ever since. This is his first fiction publication.

THE LITTLE PEOPLE by Neal Privett

The man howled like an animal.

The sound of his cries sent a collective shudder reeling through the town, rousing everyone from their fitful beds and cold-sweated nightmares. The sun rose over the dark mountains and melted into an unforgiving dawn as the prisoner wailed like a banshee in chains. His throat was so raw that the words traipsed off into hoarse emanations, a strange language more suited to a dying animal than a man. Even if that man was about to swing from a rope straight into the back country of Eternity. Or, if the townsfolk had their way...Hell.

The townsfolk rose and prepared themselves for one of the few entertainments available in the West...a hanging. This one was more than a social event, however, it was personal. The residents of Crimson Rock were good, hearty, God-fearing folks. The kind of people that had carved a home out of wilderness and weren't too fond of thieves and murderers and had a natural predilection for seeing such transgressors suffer and die, despite their good Christian values. For them, right was right and wrong was wrong. And murder was wrong. Even if it was the upstanding proprietor of the general store and the sometimes Sunday school teacher who had committed not one, but five murders, mostly women.

In the dank inner sanctum of his jail cell, John Laird screamed until his throat bled. He banged his head on the cold stone walls until his skull cracked and begged for the sheriff's belief in wild fits of panic and rage. Most people thought he had lost his mind. He had told the story in the courtroom, the same wild tale that he was found babbling, covered in blood. He unleashed the horrid narrative upon the town during the proceedings that followed; the tale of the Little People and what they had made him do. It wasn't his fault...it was the fault of faeries.

An early morning breeze blew across the dirt street as Byron Hatfield walked nervously towards the jail, two pencils and a notebook in hand. His guts quivered at the thought of interviewing a convicted murderer, but at the same time, his mind beamed with the chance to get the exclusive story, which would eventually resonate all over the territory, maybe even all the way back east. They would tell and re-tell the story of John Laird and his Little People for years to come. Someone would write a ballad...maybe even a novel for a long winter's reading. For this was no ordinary murderer. His crimes were so unutterably horrible that two girls and an old man actually fainted in the courtroom when the details were read aloud. Laird did things to his victims that were unprecedented... unholy. It was the case of the century. And he was on the very cusp of it all. Thanks to the sheriff, who was also his uncle.

The sheriff met young Hatfield at the door, unlocking it quickly and pulling him inside. "Preacher will be here shortly. You got a few minutes. Make it good. We're gonna hang the Irishman before daylight burns a hole in our hats."

Hatfield nodded and followed his uncle down a dark hallway to the cells. Laird's screams deafened him, made his heart buckle and writhe in his chest. He glanced back at his uncle and marvelled: the terrible screams of the condemned seemingly had no effect on him.

An old vagrant cowered in the corner cell, with his face pressed into a dirty pillow. He cried out frantically when he saw Hatfield. "God...please make him stop! Please!"

"Shut up, you old fool," the sheriff yelled as he banged on the bars. "We're gonna make him quiet soon enough!" The sheriff unlocked the door to Laird's cell and motioned for Hatfield to step inside. The young reporter hesitated and looked at his uncle. "Well...get in there, boy! Ain't this what you wanted? Smithy will be sittin' at the end of the hall with a rifle. We won't let this crazy son of a bitch harm you."

Hatfield gulped and moved inside the cell. The sheriff laughed and slammed the door shut, causing Hatfield to jump. "Damned if your mother would never let me hear the end of it if ole Laird there harmed a pretty little hair on your head!"

Laird stopped screaming. He sat on his bunk, staring at Hatfield. The young reporter nodded to him and called out, "Uncle Jack...could you bring me a candle? It's kinda dark in here."

"Hell, I reckon," the sheriff said. He returned in a few seconds with a candle. Opening the cell door he handed it to Hatfield. The reporter pulled up a chair and sat the candle on a nearby table. The cell was instantly illuminated, bathed in a weird light that seemed to make Laird's eyes glow and the shadows distort into dark marionettes that writhed and scratched at invisible flesh.

Hatfield noticed the dark splotches of dried blood on the wall that corresponded with the dark splotches of dried blood that plastered Laird's forehead and hair. A faint stream of red glistened from his nose as he spoke. "You a preacher?"

"No," Hatfield said. "I'm a reporter."

"You come to talk of...the...the..." Laird slammed the back of his head against the wall and screamed. Hatfield jumped from his seat and backed up to the bars. The deputy appeared and banged on them with the butt of his rifle. "Shut up, damn you!"

Laird fell immediately into a cold silence. He leaned over and glared at Hatfield for a second before a toothy grin came over his visage and he began to laugh. His voice sounded child-like and distant, as if he were a boy calling up to a person or persons unknown from the bottom of a dark well.

The deputy returned to his chair and Hatfield took out his notebook and pencil. "Tell me about them..."

"The Little People? You want to know about them?"

Laird lunged towards Hatfield. The prisoner didn't move really, he seemed to fill the space between them in a fraction of a second. Like a shadow. Hatfield took a deep breath and continued. "Yes, I do. Tell me."

Laird stared deep into Hatfield's eyes and the reporter could sense every haunted inch of the man's depthless soul. And he didn't like it. But he

continued, nonetheless.

The prisoner leaned back into his bunk as quickly as he had lunged forward. He smiled like a demon and shook his head slowly. "I ain't so sure they want me talkin' about 'em."

"What does it matter? You are gonna hang in less than hour anyway. They can't get to you now."

"That's what you think," Laird replied...fear bubbling up in his bloodshot eyes. "They will get you in this life...or in the next. They ain't human, you dumb bastard! They are from the next world and they can jump back and forth whenever they feels like it, understand?"

"I do. I will listen. Tell me what happened..."

Laird eased back into the wavering shadows and sighed. Words rolled from his obscured face and a sheath of ice formed on the young man's spine as he listened intently to the doomed prisoner and scribbled.

"I arrived in America back in '67 with a trunk bequeathed to me by my late uncle, Jeremiah. In his will he stated that I was not to open the trunk under any circumstances, but to bury it away in a hole dug deep into the earth, where it would rest until Hell itself froze over! Always an obedient lad, I did what my uncle instructed of me. I left Ireland the following spring, ready to seek my fortune in the grand States. I bought passage on a ship and weeks later, I arrived in New York. But upon the occasion of collecting my belongings, I found the trunk...the same damnable trunk, mind you, that I had buried back in Ireland. I near collapsed in bewilderment, as it was plain that it was the same trunk! I thought my uncle's spirit must've played a trick upon me, but my name was printed on the side just the same and I feared to leave it behind, so I took it with me. The trunk followed me, lad. Everywhere I went, I either buried it...or tied rocks to it and sank it in the river. I even burned it once, to no avail. I tried several times, but the damnable trunk always found its way back to me. Then I began to hear stirrings inside it. And late at night, I began to hear voices inside callin' to me!"

"Did you open it?"

"No! I dared not! Every time I tried, unsuccessfully, to rid myself of the haunted trunk, only to find it on my doorstep again. So I pushed it back into the corner of my house and covered it with a rug.

"Two years later, I found myself out here on the frontier and I got into the store business, doing mighty well for myself. I met a woman here, fell in love, and did what our omnipotent God directed every man to do...I married and settled into a domestic life of happiness. We were soon expecting."

"What became of your wife?"

A shiver came over the entire cell, a blast of unexpected cold that hit Hatfield deep in his stomach. He pulled his coat tighter around his body and continued writing, though the pencil shook in his hand. Laird coughed, then broke into retching sobs. But he gained control of himself and continued.

"The poor, poor girl. She found the trunk one day, despite my best attempts at concealing it. She enquired about the contents and I instructed her to never open it. I removed the trunk and buried it once more, out back of the house, but as always, it returned to me

the following morning and I hid it in the corner of my attic. But my wife was a curious woman and she found the trunk...and may God help me, she picked the lock and opened it...unleashing an evil, as old as the Devil himself!

"I discovered my wife one evening after returning from the store. She lay in a pool of her own blood in the attic, a look of pure terror etched across her face. That look...will follow me into the next world and beyond. My wife had seen the bowels of Hell itself...it was carved into her face by tiny claws! Our unborn child...was cut from her belly and lay beside her..."

"Good God!"

"They came to me after that...the Little People! They climbed upon my bed whenever I collapsed from exhaustion and they spoke to me!"

"What did they say?"

"Terrible things...things not of this world...things that no human should ever hear! They told me that blood was their life's milk...that I had to bring them more or the souls of my dead wife and unborn child would be forever tormented by their wrath!"

"But what happened with your wife's death? Surely there was an inquest..."

"I buried her and told everyone that she had left me for a life better than that of a storekeeper's wife."

"Describe the Little People...what are they? What do they look like?"

"They are dark faeries, lad! Not the soft voiced denizens of dreams, but their evil cousins, who come to this world not to spread magic, but to destroy! They are tiny, less than the length of a full-grown man's hand. They are covered in black or grey fur...with glowing yellow eyes and the sharp teeth of a rat. They whisper and creep behind the walls at night. Sometimes you can hear them laughing...whisperin' to one another and plotting unspeakable horrors against the good people who pray and slumber peacefully in their beds. And they reek of rot and filth. You can smell 'em throughout the house. And once they started to show themselves to me, that's when they demanded I do things for them..."

"Such as?"

"Bring them bodies to defile. First it was a woman down by the river. Then it was a school girl. Then a mule-driver from another town...I coaxed them... promised them things..."

"What did you promise them?"

"Money, mostly."

"And then what did you do?"

"I killed them all and...chopped them into pieces...squeezed the blood into bowls and fed the Little People. They came out from the walls and lapped at the hot blood like they were animals! They still talk to me...tell me that blood is sweet! They tell me that they have my wife and child in that other, faraway, land! Some of them came to me just last night!" The Irishman gestured nervously at the bars above. "They sat there and laughed at me...called me by name. They told me that they ain't through with me yet!" Laird's voice broke all of a sudden and he began to cry. "I brought 'em from the old country to this one...but by God! I never meant to!" He lunged forward again, almost knocking over the candle and clutched Hatfield's sleeve. "You believe me now, don't you?"

Hatfield carefully pried the prisoner's vice-like fingers from his coat and eased him back. "Easy, Laird. Relax. I believe you."

Laird's face lit up. "You do? Really?"

The sound of keys jangling and the cell door opening interrupted them. Laird glanced up and his eyes became enflamed with desperation when he saw the sheriff, the deputy, and a preacher filing into his cell. The sheriff motioned to Hatfield. "Your conversation about faeries is over!"

The condemned man screamed as he dove for Hatfield. "Please! Please tell them that it wasn't me! The Little People made me do it! Tell them!"

Hatfield winced as the deputy's rifle stock connected with Laird's temple, knocking him to the floor. But he did not lose consciousness. If anything, it made him wilder. He struggled against his bracelets and howled like a man possessed. The preacher tried to calm him and give him those last and final rites due all condemned prisoners on their fateful mornings, but Laird would not calm down enough to hear. He stopped his tirade long enough to gaze into Hatfield's eyes and glean the truth.

The reporter did not believe.

When that cold knowledge seeped into Laird's mind, he threw his head back and wailed again. He writhed and jumped, knocking the preacher down and upsetting the table. But it was to no avail. The sheriff and deputy were bears of men, in the frontier way, and they pulled the howling man down the hall and across the street to the waiting gallows. Hatfield watched from the doorway as the hangman pulled a bag over Laird's face and set the noose. Amidst a volley of shouts and curses from the crowd, the lever was pulled and time almost stopped as the prisoner fell through space. Then time caught up and his neck popped. The body swung limp, back and forth as the crowd cheered. And so, John Laird went to his Maker.

And he never stopped screaming.

Byron Hatfield wiped his sweaty hands on his trousers as he stood outside the Laird house. After the day's upsetting activities, he had spent a good portion of the afternoon in the local saloon with a good card game and a bottle of whiskey to help him forget the awful image of Laird burned into his psyche. Or maybe it was two bottles.

The man was a murderer...there was no doubt. But his tale of the Little People had intrigued Hatfield, and the concept of such a thing, despite the utter madness of it all, had appealed to the man of letters that he was. And so, with whiskey's encouragement and a shameless drive for fame that this story could bring, the youth ventured to the far side of the dusty town, without consulting his uncle. And here he stood...his heart pounding and the sun setting behind the jagged mountains.

The reporter pushed the bowler hat back on his head and dabbed the sweat from his face with a handkerchief. "Well...are you brave enough to go in, Hatfield, old boy?" He turned up the kerosene lantern and smiled to himself. "You are quite insane. But it's a story you want...and therein awaits the story... along with a passel of faeries or an empty house full of air." He groaned wistfully, "Or ghosts."

The reporter moved stealthily forward, towards the shadow-filled house.

The front door had been shattered. The sheriff had undoubtedly kicked it in when he arrested Laird and no one had repaired it. Hatfield pushed the door open and shone his lantern inside. The light cut through the darkness, displaying nothing extraordinary, except for the glaring fact of some missing furniture. Hatfield cursed. The self-righteous townsfolk had helped themselves to some of Laird's belongings, somehow justifying the petty theft amongst themselves, despite their earlier condemnation of the man's crimes. He moved through the parlour, into the front room. There was no table...no chairs...no sofa seat. The china cabinet was empty, devoid of its finery. He imagined the silverware was gone, too.

He picked up a framed photograph face-down on the floor. It was a studio portrait of Laird and his wife. The glass was cracked, probably from being tossed aside by an eager looter, who had not even given Laird time to grow cold. The bastards.

Hatfield moved down the hallway and stopped when he reached the stairs. They led upwards into total darkness. He wiped his mouth and thought for a long second, his resolve softening a little. But the grand old journalistic drive propelled him forward, up the dark stairs, steadily, with his lantern outstretched. His heart skipped a beat with each creaking step. A cold sweat rolled down his face and saturated his shirt. At the end of the stairs was the closed attic door.

Hatfield hesitated again. The

whiskey was beginning to wear off, and his stomach felt empty and a mile deep. He hovered there at the top of the stairs, his trembling hand holding the lantern before him...his mind debating what waited on the other side of the door. He reached out and tested it. The knob turned in his hand and he pushed the door open.

The bogeyman did not jump out at Hatfield as he feared. Instead there was nothing but an empty room, draped in lantern light and teeming with harmless shadows in the corners. He started to turn around, but something caught his eye.

A blackish splotch coated the floor in one spot. He shone his light on it and shivered. Dried blood. "That must be where his wife expired," he said to himself. Something else grabbed his attention. Over in the corner was the trunk!

Hatfield ransacked his thoughts, challenging each one. Did he dare?

He smirked. Damnation and hell, yes, he dared! He shuffled over to the trunk and with one defiant motion, he lifted the top. The aged hinges grated and creaked.

There was nothing inside.

Hatfield shook his head and laughed. Laird was mentally unstable and unwilling, or unable, to accept responsibility for his heinous crimes. That was it and all. There were no such things as Little People. The youth chastised himself for being an idiot and headed back down the stairs, closing the attic door behind him.

It was on the next to last step that the small dark object raced in front of him. It was lightning fast and when it

clipped his right foot, Hatfield fell sprawling and crashed onto the floor. The impact jarred the entire house and knocked the breath out of him. The lantern smashed into a thousand shards, covering the floor with kerosene. The youth lay there, in complete darkness, his head swirling in confusion. His hand was wet, though he could not be sure if it was kerosene or blood.

In a moment, however, he knew that his hand was bleeding, because he felt, in the darkness, a dozen unseen, miniscule, tongues lapping the liquid from his fingers. He cried out as he felt the blood being sucked from him...the tongues wagging hungrily over the stinging wound.

Tiny glowing eyes danced around him like fireflies in the darkness. He moaned as the fetid stench assaulted his nostrils. Then he heard the small voices whispering in unison, "Yes! Blood! So sweet! More!"

He was dazed...frozen to the floor. He tried to rise, but his body wouldn't obey. He heard them scurrying, like rats, all around him. They pushed through his hair, scratched his face. They whispered in his ears in harsh otherworldly voices, "You belong to us!"

Their laughter rang out louder and louder in the darkness. Hatfield struggled and cried out, praying that he could see...wishing that he could rise from the floor and run away. A savage sound caused the breath to catch in his dry throat: the unmistakable sound of something sharp and metal...a blade... opening.

The last thing Hatfield remembered, before the onslaught of blackness, was the icy, gut churning pain of a blade slicing into his flesh...his face...his fingers. The house was filled with his screams, but no one in town heard them.

A girl disappeared the next day. Three days later, another girl vanished. Parts of their dismembered corpses were found a week later floating in the river. Byron Hatfield was arrested soon after. They found him wandering in the woods, laughing like a maniac, with a blood stained straight razor bearing John Laird's initials in his hand. He was incarcerated in the town jail by his astonished uncle. The young writer had several deep running scars on his face and was missing some fingers. His eyes glowed with a demon's light and he waited in the dark of his cell, screaming about the Little People until the hangman arrived.

THE END

ABOUT THE AUTHOR

Neal Privett lives on a farm somewhere in Tennessee, where he writes furiously, drinks too much coffee, and brews horror pulp in the barn. His work can be found in several upcoming anthologies from Pro Se, Sirens Call, and Horrified Press, as well as in the magazines *Blood Moon Rising, Schlock!, Cheapjack Pulp, Sanitarium, We Belong Dead,* and *The Horror Zine.*

WOE, BABYLON BESIEGED by Mark Mellon

The moon shone full on Babylon that foredoomed night. Thousands of torches burned outside the walls. The Assyrians ringed the city round. The air rang with shouted commands and battle drums' thunder as infantry mounted a night assault. Massed ranks in chain mail and conical helmets locked shields and marched up an earthen ramp built by engineers to the outer walls' edge. Babylonian warriors hurled down stones, spears, and slingshots as the infantry advanced. They poured boiling pitch from flanking towers. Burnt, stabbed, or their skulls crushed, many Assyrians fell, only to have their comrades grimly tread over them, determined to force a breach. The greatest opportunity in their lives lay behind Babylon's walls. Once these were forced, the sack would follow with each man free to rape, rob, murder, and burn as he saw fit.

Siege equipment rumbled slowly forward. A 'horse', a four wheeled hut, was manoeuvred into place. The men inside vigorously jabbed away at the fired clay walls with a massive iron spike and soon tore open a breach. Babylonians shot flaming arrows into the horse's roof, but failed to ignite the soaking wet, raw sheep hides that covered it. Unwieldy siege towers rolled remorselessly on specially laid tracks, higher at forty cubits than Babylon's outer walls. From the fighting tops expert bowmen rained arrows down on hapless Babylonians.

Well out of range, Sennacherib, King of the Assyrians, reclined upon his upholstered palanquin and watched the destruction of the greatest and most beautiful city in the world with inexpressible joy. He gestured for a eunuch to fetch snow chilled palm wine, but capriciously dashed the jewelled gold goblet away and stood.

"Why loiter when my men fight bravely? Better to lead the assault."

He seized his bow and quiver and ran toward the walls. An infantryman grabbed a shield of thick, plaited reeds, taller than a man, and hurried before Sennacherib, expertly protecting him. Resplendent in his imperial purple, gold fringed tunic, Sennacherib nocked an arrow, pulled, and released. As suddenly as he conceived it, Sennacherib lost interest. He returned to his palanquin to his eunuchs' relief.

"Soon, Samsu-iluna will be on his knees before me."

His eunuchs squealed with sycophantic, high pitched laughter. What could be more delightful than to see the once mighty King of Babylon laid low and defeated, his city in flaming ruins, only at the start of his misery, pain, degradation, and ultimate, horrible death?

Samsu-iluna ran down the tunnel that went beneath the Purattu river, kilt hiked up around his knees. Sweat poured down his shaven head, smeared the kohl around his eyes. Fat and inactive, Samsu-iluna nonetheless hurried to Babylon's eastern half, accompanied by Rimush, captain of his guard, ten warriors, and Nidintu-Bel, Priest of Baal-Shem-Nibburath, personally fetched by Samsu-iluna from his seldom visited underground temple.

"God King, are you sure this is wise?"

"Quiet, priest. I know what I'm doing. Did you bring the tablets?"

"In my tunic sleeves, God King."

They reached the tunnel's end, ascended the stairs, and stood in the Esagila's courtyard. They were safe for the moment behind the temple's solid brass doors. Muffled by the tunnel, the noise from the siege in the courtyard was an overwhelming, ear shattering mix of screams, roars, drumbeats, and the constant, sinister shuffle only tens of thousands of marching feet made. Abd-ili, High Priest of Marduk, awaited as Samsu-iluna had ordered, guarded by more warriors. Their presence reassured Samsu-iluna. At least his authority still held good here.

Dignified in his long, fringed kilt and cape, thick, hennaed beard woven into tresses, Abd-ili bowed low, rose, and frowned. He pointed at Nidintu-Bel.

"It's forbidden for him to set foot within the Esagila. He defiles Marduk's house."

Samsu-iluna struck Abd-ili in the face. The priest reeled from the blow.

"Quiet. I decide what's forbidden. Are the Awellum's children assembled?"

Face red, a chastened Abd-ili nodded. "Yes, God King. Young men and women of the noblest houses, fifteen each, taken to the Tower as you commanded. But what is the purpose? I know no rite that involves—"

Samsu-iluna raised his hand again and Abd-ili cowered.

"Quiet. The sacrificial rite is Nidintu-Bel's business. Do you understand?"

Abd-ili drew himself to his full height and spoke with hardly a tremor.

"That's blasphemy, God King. You outrage Marduk and will surely pay."

"Rimush."

The bronze blade cut Abd-ili

nearly in two. He wailed and fell to the ground, entrails trailing.

"Take me to the summit."

"Yes, God King."

The outer walls were breached now in several places. Towers burned while Babylonian defenders doggedly fought on. There was a portentous thud. A battering ram crashed against the Gate of Urash. The iron bars that held the gate in place groaned from the strain. A few more blows and they would certainly give way.

Nahro the division commander raced on a horse up to Sennacherib. He halted the galloping animal, dismounted, ran to his monarch, and prostrated himself.

"King of Kings, Lord of Hosts, King of Assur, the Gate of Urash will soon be breached. Babylon's fall is imminent. The Division of Harran awaits your orders."

With a great shout of exaltation, Sennacherib leapt from his palanquin. He sneered at Babylon's lofty outer walls, already partially enveloped in flames.

"Who will defend you now, Babylon? Where are your mighty gods now? Samsu-iluna, my feet shall tread upon your neck. You'll be my footstool."

He turned to Nahro. "Here are my orders. Throw down the city and its houses from the foundations to the roofs. Ravage the women and burn everything. Tear down the outer and inner walls, destroy the temples, especially the Esagila. Smash all their idols and throw them into the Puratta. Let them be carried to the sea. And

massacre the population. Let no one survive."

Nahro beamed at this display of manly Assyrian ferocity. He rose and bowed.

"As you command, Mighty King. Before the night is done, pyramids of severed heads will be set up before Babylon's gates."

Nahro rode off. Sennacherib lay on his palanquin.

"More wine."

The Tower of Babel, tallest building in the world, consisted of seven different coloured storeys, surmounted by Marduk's blue Sanctuary. Samsu-iluna and the others hurried up a side staircase that flanked the ceremonial Grand Stairway. The climb only added to Samsu-iluna's stress. Each step was leaden agony. Rimush draped an arm over his shoulders and helped Samsu-iluna. Babylon lay spread before them, the bright moon reflected in the Puratta, flames on the outer walls, and everywhere, in all directions, flickering Assyrian torches.

Disconsolate wails rose up, pitiful moans, sobs, and lamentations from men, women, and children, bereft by the certain knowledge that only ruin and death awaited on the morrow. Their cries cut Samsu-iluna like a knife. He looked skyward and asked Marduk yet again.

"Why? How have I failed you?"

Yet as with each prior fervent appeal, the sky remained silent. Marduk had deserted Samsu-iluna and Babylon, left him and his people to fend for themselves against the Assyrians. If he was taken captive, Samsu-iluna would be led through Nineveh with a ring through his nose like a bull, displayed in a cage like a monkey, and finally have his hands, feet, nose, and ears cut off with cleavers by jailers before they tore out his tongue and eyes with red hot pincers. This fate awaited after Sennacherib made him watch his city burn, his people massacred, and his idols destroyed.

Defeat was certain. The Assyrians had already breached the outer walls. Yet another choice still remained, a mean, miserable one, but still a choice. Samsu-iluna could take the revenge of the vanquished. If he reached the Tower's top and if Nidintu-Bel could properly work his incantations. He looked behind. The old priest had physically failed long ago. Two warriors carried him up the stairs.

"Hurry, Rimush."

They reached the second storey and ran to another side staircase. Sharp pain rhythmically pulsed in Samsu-iluna's stomach. At the second storey's top, the Hanging Gardens came into view. Flaming, pitch tipped arrows arced over the walls into the terraces. Once verdant palms, fruit, almond, and olive trees blazed in the night, quickly burned to a crisp. Like everything else, the green Paradise where Samsu-iluna spent so many happy moments over the years among scented terraces with his wives and concubines, was ruined by the Assyrians.

"By my own genitals I swear, Sennacherib, I'll take you with me."

The Gate of Urash's portals lay broken, torn aside by the Assyrians in their frenzy to take Babylon. Soon after, the Gate of Ishtar fell. Gold and yellow bulls and dragons stood bright against the blue tiles by flames' light. Infantry hustled through the open gates only to find themselves trapped between the inner and outer walls on narrow, open ground, ideal targets.

Stones and pottery fell on the Assyrians. Aware the inner walls were their last defence, the Babylonians fought with desperate courage and determination. Men fell with battered skulls and broken bones.

Battle hardened, accustomed to reverses and crises, the Assyrians quickly rebounded. Scaling ladders were propped against walls. Chain mail glittered in the fire as the Assyrians scuttled up the ladders like a horde of malignant beetles, shields held overhead for protection.

Babylonians smashed Assyrians' heads with stone maces as they crested the walls, pitched over ladders so Assyrians fell to their deaths by the score, slashed off fingers that clutched at parapets, and fought on, against hope, against reason, beyond the limit of human endurance, until breath was wrenched from their chests in ragged, sobbing heaves.

And still infantry poured through the open gates in steadily increasing numbers, indifferent to dead comrades for that only meant more loot. They mounted an organized, disciplined attack on the walls from all sides. The sheer number of ladders and men on them simply overwhelmed the Babylonians. Warriors fought to the death on the ramparts, hacked and slashed at Assyrians only to be stabbed by spears and thrown over the walls. Wild, triumphant screams went up from Assyrians on the ramparts, savage gloats of raw, inhuman glee at Babylon's coming misery.

Other Assyrians, skilled swimmers, floated on inflated goat skins down the Puratta and infiltrated Babylon. Once inside the walls, they climbed onto the piers that supported the bridge between the city's halves, and charged the inner gates. They died in great numbers, but pinned down more warriors Babylon couldn't spare.

A great wail went up from the populace who crowded Babylon's narrow streets in happier times, goldsmiths, millers, brewers, and barbers, now doomed to slavery at best or death after degradation at the cruel Assyrians' hands. They rent their garments, tore their hair, poured ashes upon themselves, and beseeched Marduk for rescue.

And Sennacherib laughed to hear such pitiable misery. Drunk on victory and palm wine, he held his goblet high in a toast to his marauding infantry.

"None excels us in siege-craft. Truly Ashur blesses me. If any escape, have them crawl before me on all fours to humbly beg my pardon and then crucify them along the road to Nineveh."

"As you command, O King of Kings," the eunuchs responded, almost on tiptoe with anticipation. Soon, Samsu-iluna would be dragged before them, a gold ring through his bleeding nose, naked, ashamed, forced to beg for mercy.

Samsu-iluna stood on the Tower's summit by Marduk's sanctuary, a blue square topped by curved horns on each corner. A solid gold statue of Marduk ten cubits high stood inside the sanctuary. Samsu-iluna ignored his supreme deity, focused on Nidintu-Bel. The priest sat on a guard's back, drank water from a flask, and gasped for air. Samsu-iluna's own heart pounded against his ribcage. His temples throbbed as if about to explode. A powerful urge to simply give up swept over him, to lie down and die.

Samsu-iluna forced himself to act.

"Priest. Pull yourself together. Perform the rites now."

"God King, I know the liturgy. At least, I think I do, but I've never read it aloud."

"Rimush, cut off his ears."

"No, God King. I can perform the rites. Just give me a torch to read by."

"Good. Rimush. Take us to the Awellum's children."

At the whitewashed storey's edge, thirty sons and daughters of Babylon's richest noble families knelt in two ranks, surrounded by warriors each armed with a stone mace. They wore their best finery, the women in red headdresses, emeralds and pearls, the men with gold diadems and imperial purple tunics. Eyes glazed in a potent, synergetic stupor, barely able to hold up their heads, drool hung from several mouths. A priest highly skilled in potions had administered a stiff dose of opium mixed with palm wine.

"Read the tablets, Nidintu-Bel."

Nidintu-Bel reached into a trailing sleeve and removed three small, fired clay tablets covered with cuneiform ideograms, curious indentations like chicken tracks. Battered and chipped at the edges, they were obviously of great age, the work of some Sumerian scribe in the time of Ur of the Chaldees. A guard held a torch close so old, nearly-blind eyes could read.

"When I say 'selah,' a guard must do his part. It's essential. This is understood?" Nidintu-Bel quavered.

"Yes, hurry. We don't have much time."

Nidintu-Bel held a tablet to his nose and recited. Strange, distorted, polysyllabic words streamed forth, crude transcriptions into Sumerian, dead writing of a language no human tongue was ever meant to speak.

"Ph'nglui mglw'nafh Baal-Shem-Nibburath Pnath wgah'nagl fhtagn."

A curious chill ran over Samsu-iluna. Hairs prickled along his spine.

"Selah."

A guard brought down a heavy mace with all his strength and cracked a young noble's skull, killed him with one blow. He slumped over as blood seeped from his shattered head. In a drugged trance, the others sat motionless.

"Ch'yar ul'nyar Baal-Shem-Nibburath. Selah."

A young woman was bludgeoned. Nidintu-Bel worked his way through the incomprehensible verses. At each line's end, another aristocrat was sacrificed until a wide pool of black blood formed. Meanwhile, the Assyrian assault intensified. Infantry were inside the inner walls in increasing numbers. They cut people down in the streets and dragged women out by their hair to rape them. At any moment, they'd storm the Esagila. Samsu-iluna grew increasingly agitated. He fought to stay silent while Nindintu-Bel read the last tablet.

"Mglw'nafh fhthagn-ngah cf'ayak 'vulgtmm vugtlag'n, Baal-Shem-Nibburath cf'tagn. Selah."

The last body fell. Samsu-iluna looked expectantly around, yet saw nothing but rapine and plunder and Assyrian infantry headed toward the Esagila, torches in hand, plainly bent upon arson. He looked to the sky and the plains beyond, but there was nothing, no hint of intervention.

"Nindintu-Bel, you miserable, lying old fool, you've tricked me. Rimush, cut him into pieces and throw them over the side."

"No, God King. Please—"

A strange, thin piping interrupted, mysterious, atonal music of an utterly alien kind from an undetectable source. The pipes grew louder until they became an awful, cacophonous, staccato wail that drowned out the Assyrian war drums. Strange lights pulsed in the sky, gauzy, intertwined clouds of unearthly colours that irked and tortured human eyes. Confronted by the unknown, stalwart infantrymen blanched in terror. The awful, headlong, Assyrian onslaught stopped dead. The army stood transfixed and awestruck by the cosmic rupture, no more powerful now than ants in an earthquake's grip. Babylonians as well were in dread as the colours grew more intense and the music louder and shriller.

"For the love of Marduk, will no one save us?"

The Puratta foamed between Babylon's halves, a roiling whirlpool that spun at incredible speed. A huge black and purple tentacle shot forth from the seething waters. The enormous, sucker covered arm smashed down onto Babylon's eastern half, pulverized everything and everyone in its path,

17

Babylonian and Assyrian alike. Another tentacle fell onto the western half with equally devastating results. An amorphous, shadowy monster pulled itself from the Puratta, the mountain sized head infested with multiple mouths ringed with fangs and hooded eyes that burned malignant blue. Nindintu-Bel cried out with professional joy at his vindication even though it meant certain doom.

"Behold, God King. Baal-Shem-Nibburath, Lord of the Lands beyond Irkalla Kur."

More tentacles snaked out. They grabbed people by the thousands and jammed them into Baal-Shem-Nibburath's multiple ravenous maws. As he ate, Baal-Shem-Nibburath grew in size and darkness until the monster loomed over Babylon, greater than the Tower of Babel. A bilious blue eye looked dead into Samsu-iluna's. A tentacle reached out. The King of Babylon showed no fear.

"Yes. It's the bargain I made. But take Sennacherib too. Let him die with me."

Exhalations of rotting flesh, sickly coughs of cynical laughter poured from multiple mouths. A tentacle sailed over Babylon, straight and sure as a well-aimed arrow. Before Sennacherib's eyes could even widen in surprise, a sucker slapped down and lifted him from his palanquin.

"Ashur, save me," he screamed as the tentacle guided him toward a grinding maw.

"Yes, pray to your god. He'll save you," Samsu-iluna laughed as he went feet first into another mouth.

And all the others in Babylon fell prey in turn to Baal-Shem-Nibburath's unquenchable hunger, from Nindintu-Bel to the least slave. Warrior or merchant, woman or babe, whether they cowered behind walls or ran to hide in the fields, the tentacles slithered into each hiding place and dragged victims away kicking and screaming until in the end, no one was left but Baal-Shem-Nibburath, bulk taller than the sky, ruler of an empty domain.

And Babylon shall become a heap of ruins, the haunting place of dragons, a horror and a hissing, without an inhabitant.

THE END

```
        ABOUT THE AUTHOR

  Mark Mellon is a novelist who
supports his family by working as
an attorney. Short fiction of his
has recently appeared in Hinnom,
Mythaxis, and Infernal Ink. Four
  of his novels and over sixty
short stories have been published
in the USA, UK, Ireland, and Den-
mark. A novella, Escape from Byz-
antium, won the 2010 Independent
Publisher Silver Medal for F/SF.
A website featuring his writing
is at www.mellonwritesagain.com
```

THE SKUDDA by Sam Graham

"Jack, why don't you come and sit here, a bit closer to Mummy?" Sarah patted the cushion beside her. Jack glanced over, but stayed perched on the edge at the far side of the sofa. She saw his lip tremble. His small hands clenched into fists.

"I know you can hear me," she said playfully, hoping to make him laugh and distract him from whatever was bothering him. "I can see you looking.

See, you just did it again. Come here, darling." She reached over and touched his shoulder, but her son flinched away. Sarah retracted her hand. The playfulness was gone. "Sweetie, what's the matter?"

Nothing.

"Jack, what is it? Tell mummy now, please."

"What for?" the six year old muttered. He turned away from her.

Sarah struggled to keep the concern out of her voice. "Because I've hardly seen you in the last few days. You've barely said two words to me and you've spent all your time after school up in your room lately. I miss you, that's all. I thought you might like to cuddle while we watch a film together?" She held out her arms and after a moment's hesitation, Jack shuffled over and nestled his head on her chest. Sarah leaned back into the couch cushions. "I love you, you know?" she said. Jack made a noise, a quiet mumbling. Sarah felt his whole body trembling. She kissed the top of his head and with her free hand, stroked his hair, afraid to ask the question that was plaguing her mind.

Does he know? Oh god I've been so careful.

A cold feeling pooled in the pit of her stomach. He couldn't have found out.

But she didn't ask him. She was afraid he'd say yes, and if he didn't know, letting it slip by mentioning it was the worst thing she could think of. So they each sat in silence as they watched TV. Just the two of them on the four-seater that felt too big and empty for them now. The whole time the question plagued her. And when Jack began to

whimper softly, still trembling under her arm, she didn't move, nor try to comfort him, afraid what he'd say was upsetting him.

She hated herself for her indecision. It brought her to tears too, but she didn't let him see it. They both pretended not to notice each other. Neither spoke until the film had finished.

Sarah roused from a troubled sleep and cracked one eye open. The room was pitch black, not time to get up yet. She reached over to the other side of the bed, expecting to wrap her arm around warm skin and let the steady rise and fall of Kieran's breathing carry her back to sleep. But her eyes opened wide when she touched nothing but cold, flat sheets. Memories of that night flooded her mind, flashes of colour amidst the chaos. The blue lights from the ambulance. The green jackets on the paramedics. The lifeless stare in Kieran's eyes.

That side of the bed had been empty for weeks. It was just her bed now.

She lay awake until morning.

Jack sat waiting at the kitchen table. He watched as his mum took three plates from the cupboard, paused, then put one back. She turned away from him as she cried.

She hadn't got used to cooking for just the two of them yet and out of habit she'd made enough food for three. After drying her eyes she divided the shepherd's pie into two large portions, took them over to the table and sat down. She watched her son stir the mashed potatoes for five minutes before eating the tiniest morsel and putting his fork down. But she wasn't eating either. That cold feeling in her stomach left no room for food. She looked for something in Jack's actions to dispel her fears, but everything she saw only made them worse. Now she was more convinced that he knew. And still she was afraid to ask. That cold feeling grew.

It took Jack fifteen minutes to eat two more clumps of potato and a thin strand of mince before leaving the table. He ran up to his room, leaving Sarah alone, head rested in her hands, neither eating nor thinking about anything specific as both plates went cold. She hated herself for making too much, for forgetting, for still living in the past. Kieran was dead and he wasn't coming back, so she had to get used to it fast. She told herself to put it in the freezer for another day.

Jack can't go through this. He mustn't know.

But the change in him was obvious to her now. Despite all her attempts to hide it, not mention it around him, making up a story as to where Kieran was, Jack had found out. She didn't know how; only that this was another one of her failures.

It was another hour before Sarah moved from the table. She forgot to freeze the pie. It went in the bin the next morning.

What am I going to do?

Sarah's bare feet padded on the soft carpet, taking care to avoid the creaky floorboards as she crept towards Jack's room. Though the door was closed, she could hear him talking to his toys, making up voices for them. She leaned toward the door and listened. Hearing him play like a normal, healthy, six year old relieved her in a way she never thought it could. The elation of hearing something normal was so sudden it brought tears to her eyes. A light in the darkness of the last few months. It was salvation for Jack and in some part, herself. She didn't notice it, but that cold feeling shrank away.

"Give us the money now, or you'll be as dead as Jack's dad," one of the toys said through Jack.

What?

Sarah gasped as that cold feeling reached up for her heart. She couldn't breathe. The light was snuffed out and she was falling. Only a single thought remained; a sense of loss, of failure, of death. She was drowning. That cold feeling was a black ocean and she had sunk down into the bottom of it, the same as that night when two paramedics in green jackets informed her Kieran couldn't be revived. He was on the bed beside her. Blue lights from the ambulance outside reflected in his eyes. His arm lay outstretched towards her, hand open like he was beckoning her to hold it, but it was not him. He was no longer there. The paramedics took the body away.

She dragged herself over to the wall and sat up against it, weeping for the loss of her husband and of her son's innocence, both snuffed out too soon.

"I know it was selfish, Kieran," she whispered, "to deny him his mourning. I knew it was wrong when I first lied to him, but he's just too young to suffer it. I thought he wouldn't understand. The hole it would leave in him." She cupped her face in her hands. "I planned to tell him in a year or so. I just—" She struggled to breathe. "There's only me now and whatever I decide might end up being the wrong decision. I don't know what to do. I've failed everyone. I'm so sorry, Kieran."

In that moment Sarah wished she couldn't feel anything, but she still felt regardless.

She cried in that spot until exhaustion carried her to sleep. Even though it seemed she'd only closed her eyes for a moment, it was daylight when she woke. She was still sitting against the wall. Looking in Jack's bedroom, she found him asleep on the floor with his toys spread around him. He looked peaceful, untempered by the nightmares that affected her. Sarah envied him, but she knew his peace was momentary. Only whilst asleep would he not suffer.

She had to do something. It was just the two of them from now on and Jack was her responsibility. She couldn't wallow any longer and she couldn't let Jack be dragged down into that black ocean with her. His problems were hers to fix. She made a promise to Kieran right then.

"Jack." She sat down beside him and whispered. His eyes shifted open. "Morning, sweetie. How about, after breakfast, I was thinking that we pack a bag each and go away to the seaside for a few days?"

It was the first smile she'd seen in days. She smiled too.

The coast was only a half hour drive and being off-season made it easy to find a B&B at short notice. They spent whole days on the beach and whole evenings by the hotel's wood burner. They talked about the day's adventures and made up stories about the sea until, exhausted, he fell asleep in her arms. She sat like that for hours, staring

off into the flames, finding comfort in the warmth of his touch and his shallow, precious breathing. The solace she felt from his small hands holding on to her shifted her focus to what she still had, rather than what she'd lost.

Jack's favourite thing that week was to explore the rocks further down the beach at the mouth of the South Caves. Where they weren't covered in seaweed, the rocks were black and smoothed by the constant tides and could be treacherous if one didn't look what one was doing. When the tide was out, and after a couple of supervised trips, Sarah let him go off on his own, but made sure he stayed in sight and didn't go in the caves. Only once did he disappear, but as she rushed over, he came clambering back over the rocks, carrying his yellow bucket, eager to show her the two tiny white crabs he'd caught inside. He said someone called Eric told him where to find them.

"Jack, dear, what have I told you about talking to strangers?"

"He isn't a stranger, mummy." Jack smiled, preoccupied with the crabs scurrying around in his bucket.

"Oh, it's another little boy then. That's alright, I suppose. But be careful."

"I will, Mummy."

Jack was sad when Sarah made him release the crabs at the end of the day, but he understood why they couldn't live in the bathroom sink as he'd suggested.

That whole week Sarah didn't answer her phone, or check messages once. No visitors, no friends or neighbours, no colleagues, or teachers offering their condolences, or giving that look that they gave. They removed themselves from society and enveloped themselves solely in each other. They felt like new people, free from the burdens of their old selves, ready to move on together.

That cold feeling retreated and bothered her no more. By the end of the week Sarah had her first unbroken sleep since Kieran died. Two days later, she only took two plates out of the cupboard.

"Mummy, can we go back to the seaside this weekend?" Jack said as he buckled his seatbelt.

"Not this weekend, I'm afraid. Mummy's got some work to do. Besides, it's only been a few weeks. We'll see about half term though, OK?" Sarah said, looking at Jack in the rear-view mirror. Jack smiled at her. "By the way, who were you talking to, sweetie?"

"When?"

"When I was pulling up in the school carpark a moment ago. You were talking to someone."

"No one, Mummy. Just Eric."

"Oh, someone in your class, is it? I didn't see anyone there."

Jack kept staring at the opposite side of the table when he thought his mum wasn't looking.

"Jack, eat your food, please. It'll get cold," Sarah said.

He did as he was told, but as he ate he continued glancing at the empty chair to Sarah's left.

"What is it?"

Jack looked sheepish, trying to suppress a laugh.

"What's so funny? You might as well tell me."

Jack giggled. "He keeps making faces at me."

"Who does?" Sarah looked at the empty chair, then back at her son who was laughing uncontrollably. She hadn't noticed it before, but the chair on her left was moved away from the table like it was reserved for someone. "Jack, who are you talking about?"

"Eric."

Sarah smiled and nodded along. In the weeks since the seaside, she'd read about kids dealing with grief in hope to prepare herself, so she was expecting some unusual behaviour. This 'Eric' was par for the course, apparently. An imaginary friend was just an outlet. A way for his still-developing mind to process the events in a safe way. Jack was an only-child and they lived miles away from his school friends. No cousins to play with and he was the only kid his age on the street, so it made perfect sense. The idea of him talking to no one unsettled her, but she figured she'd soon brush it off. Jack was happy, which was all that mattered. Besides, he's just playing a game, she thought. It won't last long.

Sarah sighed. "How long is Eric going to be staying with us?" She made a point not to look at the empty seat to her left. Jack dropped his fork with a surprised clang.

"Why?"

"Well, just because he's been with us for a month now. I thought he might like to move on. Maybe see the rest of the village?" Or another part of the country?

Jack's face dropped. "But he's my friend."

"I know, darling. You two are inseparable. I mean, he comes everywhere with us now." She forced a smile.

"He said he really likes it here and wants to stay forever."

Sarah choked. "And who says I'll let him stay that long?"

Jack hopped off his chair and ran behind Eric's. "Don't make him leave, mum. He's my best friend." He patted the back of the chair, but he was no longer looking at it. He was staring over her shoulder at the top of the bookshelf. She followed his gaze to the antique ballerina statue on the top shelf. There was nothing else there... But as she turned back to her son, she caught the fabric of the ballerina's dress in the corner of her eye. It was moving, as though something had moments ago brushed against it.

"Um, Eric can stay then, in that case." Sarah said offhand, distracted by the ornament. Jack went back to his chair and continued eating.

"Mummy?"

"Yes?"

"Eric said he'd like some food too."

"But Eric can't eat, dear. I didn't make enough."

"Don't be silly, Mummy."

"Me being silly? Remember who lets Eric stay here."

"Sorry. His food is invisible. He just needs a plate to eat it off."

"So you want me to get him an empty plate and just put it there on the table?"

Jack nodded. Sarah sighed and fetched a plate. As she was on her way back, Jack reminded her about cutlery, so she went back and got a knife and fork and set them down at either side.

"Thank you, Mummy. There you go, Eric. You can eat with us every night now." Jack was happy.

But Sarah stared at that empty plate beside her. At that vacant chair that would never be sat in. Waiting for someone. Someone who was missing. Someone who wasn't coming back. Blue lights. Green coats. An empty hand. A once cold, black ocean began to fill.

She began waking up again after that.

"Mum?" Jack tugged at the hem of Sarah's skirt. "Mummy?"

Sarah paused while she balanced on the chair. "One minute. I'm nearly done hanging this up."

"Eric asked if he can have some cake tomorrow, too?"

"Sure. Whatever he wants," she said absently, focussing on standing upright on a wooden chair and trying to hang a banner for Jack's birthday party on the living room wall. Parents were told to bring their kids at nine tomorrow morning, so it all had to be done by tonight.

He lives here rent bloody free, why not eat our food as well, she thought as she taped one corner up. A phase, she'd told herself once. Just a phase. A coping strategy. No one ever said it would last nearly a year.

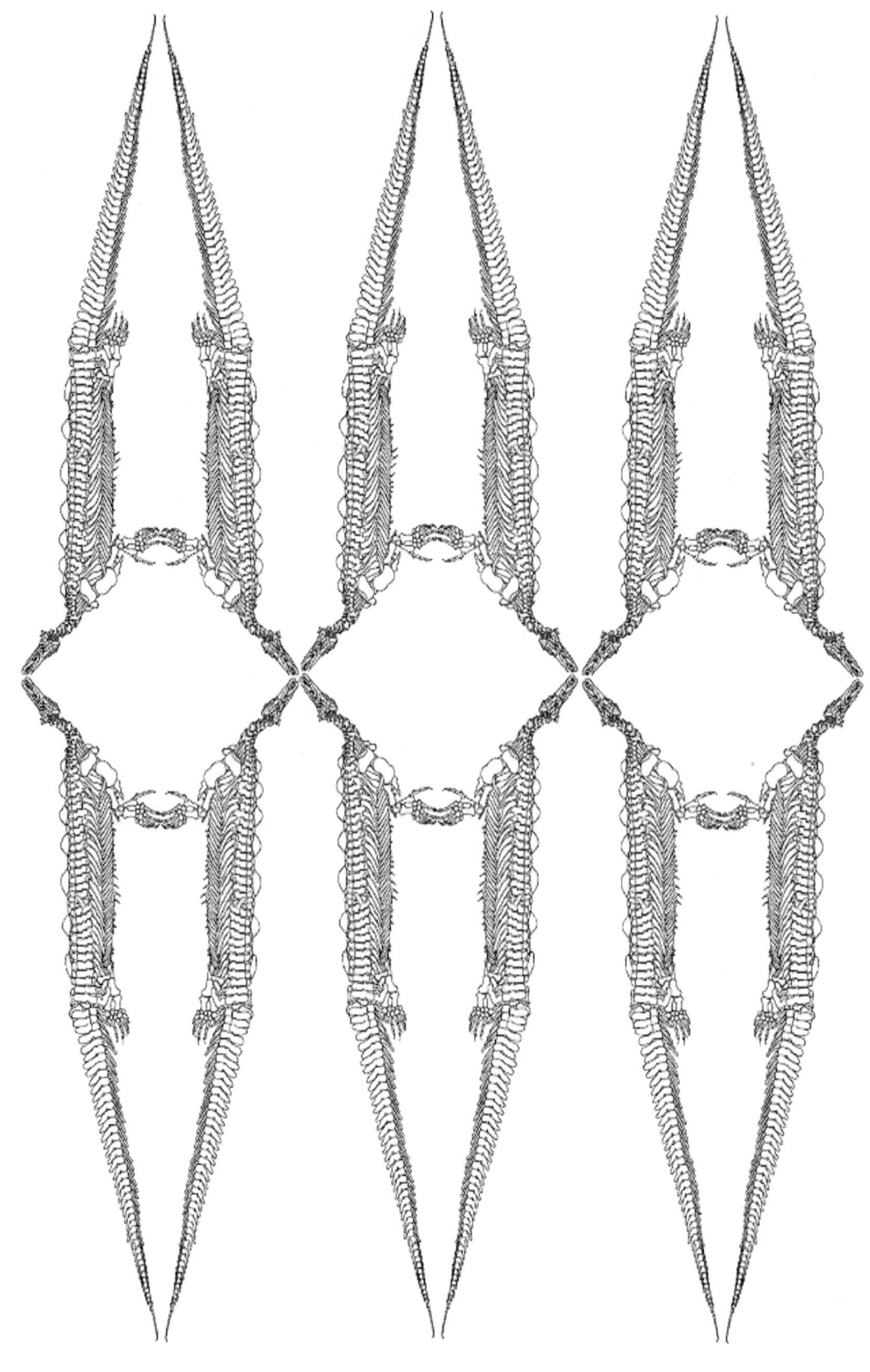

Dean Wirth

And then there was the language. She shuddered whenever she thought about it. Jack never spoke it when he knew she was listening, but the wall between their bedrooms was thin. It wasn't words per se; just a bunch of sucking sounds, clicks and hisses; too harsh and primitive to come from the mind of a normal six year old.

Reaching over for the other side of the banner, she felt the chair wobble ever so slightly. She froze and leaned against the wall to steady herself.

"Eric said I'll like being seven, Mummy. I can't wait. Mum? Mummy, look."

Sarah craned her neck to face him and as she turned, the chair tipped. Her body twisted the other way and she went over. A roll of tape flung from her hand and she reached out instinctively to grab something, anything, as the floor rushed towards her.

The carpet did nothing to cushion the fall. Her hip took most of the impact. Another thud came straight after, followed by Jack screaming.

As she sat up and massaged the pain in her side, she saw Jack was holding his head. His face was cherry red and tears streamed down his cheeks. The roll of tape had hit his head and now lay on the floor next to him. Jack held his arms out, wanting her to pick him up, but she retracted away. She was in too much pain herself. He'd caused her to fall. Him and his Eric. She was dizzy thanks to Eric, and it could have been much worse if she'd have fallen a different way. She could feel a bruise already taking shape. The nerves were on fire. God knows how long it would take to heal. She might have even fractured something. If he hadn't been pestering her about that god damn Eric all the time, none of it would have happened. Eric this, Eric that, all day and all night, every time he opened his bloody mouth.

"Oh, stop crying," she snapped.

"But Mummy—"

"No 'buts', Jack. You did this. You were pulling at my clothes and getting in my way after I distinctly told you not to. If you got hurt then it's your own fault." She tried to stand, but the pain in her hip kept her on the floor.

"But Eric said—"

"No! I don't want to hear about it. It's time to stop all the Eric talk. It's nearly eight months now. You're seven tomorrow and it's time you grew out of it." Jack's lip quivered. "Besides, you don't even need an imaginary friend when you've got real ones coming over tomorrow. And your cousin Natalie's coming too."

"Eric's not made up."

"He is! He's completely made up."

"He isn't!"

"Right, well, show him to me then. Right now, point him out to me and if he's not made up, I'll see him, won't I?" Jack wiped his nose with his hand and pointed to the stairs behind Sarah. She turned, wincing, but determined to prove her point. "See. There's nothing there, Jack. He's not real."

"But he moved just then when you turned around. He said he doesn't want you to see him."

"And why not?"

"He said you'll get scared."

"What?" She was startled, thrown off course. A moment passed and Sarah

25

sighed. Her anger was all used up and it had left her exhausted, but she sighed for a different reason.

The time had come to tell him.

"I know why you make him up, Jack. I'm sorry I didn't tell you. Your dad isn't working abroad. He's gone. He died." The boy's lip quivered. Sarah's followed. "Please don't be mad at me. I didn't tell you because I didn't want you to be upset. After going through it all myself, I just, I couldn't bear to do it all again with you. I'm sorry, son. Mummy made a mistake. And she's so, so sorry." They both sobbed. Sarah, because she'd finally admitted the truth she kept even from herself, and Jack, because having the words out there now made it real.

Between the sobs, Jack muttered again that Eric was real, but Sarah just shook her head. "He's not. He really isn't. Please Jack, stop this nonsense. It's driving mummy crazy. It's just me and you from now on, but it's going to be alright. I promise I'll make it alright. Come here." She opened her arms, but Jack stayed where he was. He glowered at her in anger, his cheeks moist from the tears, his small hands balled into fists.

"Jack, come here, sweetie."

"No."

"I beg your pardon?"

"No!" he screamed. "Eric's real. He told me what happened. He said he's seen you crying at night."

Sarah, hurt, pointed to the stairs. "You go to your room right now and stay there until tomorrow. There's no party now. I'm cancelling it, now move!" Jack ran. He screamed and stamped his feet up every step. "And no more of this 'Eric' shit, you hear me? It stops now.

And you're going to stop sleeping on the floor as well. Eric's not real, so he doesn't need your bed," she shouted. Jack responded by slamming his bedroom door as hard as he could.

Sarah wept. She hadn't meant to fly off the handle. She hadn't expected Jack to reject her like that. It hurt. What did he mean, Eric told him what happened? It made no sense. Jack must have woken up and heard her in the middle of the night. It hadn't gone away. Every night when she set an empty plate at the table, that cold feeling pooling in her stomach grew a little larger. Well, not any more. Whenever Jack mentioned his little friend she'd make a point to stop him. It was the only way to get rid of him. Blow out the match as soon as it was lit.

"Goodbye, Eric," she said to herself, and no sooner had the words left her mouth, something smashed in the dining room. She eased herself up and limped through to find her antique ballerina in pieces on the floor. She looked around, confused. Jack was still crying upstairs. The dining room was empty.

Then came the sound.

It was close. Right beside her ear. An insectile chittering. That same voice Jack made when he spoke to Eric in secret. Sarah spun round, but saw nothing. Then it came again, behind her. She turned. Nothing.

"Skudda. Skudda skudda. Skudda skudda. Skuddakuddakuddakudda..." The voice darted around her, coming from different parts of the room. Sarah spun so fast trying to track it she made herself dizzy. Wisps of movement fluttered in her peripheral vision, trails of a shadow against the light, but as soon as she looked straight at it, it was gone and the voice was coming from some-where else. Her heart raced. The dizzi-ness and the pain in her hip made her nauseous. It wasn't until she panicked and screamed for it to stop that the room fell silent.

Then she heard tiny feet padding up the stairs. Jack's bedroom door opened and her son said hello to Eric.

Sarah stood, stark frozen, trem-bling. Her lungs burned. Her heart beat so hard against her ribs it hurt. Suddenly she moved. She bolted up the stairs to Jack's room and flung the door open, dreading what she would find. But Jack was sitting innocuously with a pile of blocks. Nothing was out of place. He looked up at her, still upset, but the an-ger from before gone.

"Don't be mad, mummy, but Eric said he'll sleep in your bed tonight. I told him he's not allowed in mine any-more."

Sarah was aware she shouldn't have been driving so fast, but at that moment she didn't give a damn what the signs said; the roads were empty and she knew them like the back of her hand anyway. The forest on her left went on for another mile or so, then the road would slope downwards and flatten off half a mile outside the town. She hadn't seen another car for ten minutes as she gunned down the straight road. She wanted to go faster, get away quicker, but the rain was beating against the wind-screen and the wipers could only just cope as it was.

The twin lights of an oncoming car appeared in front of her. The sight broke her out of her reverie and she slowed down. As soon as it had passed

she looked in the mirror to see if Eric was in the car with them.

"No, mummy. You left him at home," Jack said timidly. Sarah felt the immediate panic disappear. He'd been quiet ever since she'd scooped him off the bedroom floor, bundled him in the car and drove off into the night without telling him why.

After reaching the town, she pulled up in a carpark by the seafront, turned the engine off and left the wipers run-ning. The tide was all the way in and the beach where they'd spent that peaceful week was submerged by the black sea. Moonlight shot across the tide in a thin streak of mercury and she saw the water before her now was ominous and angry. Ice-cold waves battered against the sea-wall, threatening to engulf her car. Sarah opened her window a few inches and let in the sound of the waves crashing against the seawall. From the backseat, Jack asked what they were doing there.

"We're just going to sleep here in the car tonight, sweetheart. Take your belt off and lay down across the seats. There's a good boy."

He was hesitant, but the sound of the water soon carried him off to sleep. Sarah watched the waves, trying to de-cide what to do, until she too drifted off.

But what Sarah hadn't seen when she'd asked if Eric was in the car, was her son looking over at the seat beside him before giving her an answer.

The car was beeping. The alarm sound of a door left open.

Sarah roused, hip sore but man-ageable, and turned around to see the backseat was empty. The rear door was open. In that instant she was wide awake. She got out of the car and looked around for him. The clouds were a sheet of uniform grey, the sun was rising somewhere. The rain had eased, but was still coming down sparingly. The tide was being pulled back out, but not without a fight as salty mist permeated the air.

She called out Jack's name. No answer. No people around, either, it was so early. Then she saw the blood on the back seat and her heart sank. It was a thin smear on the door handle. There was more on the tarmac beside the car and more some feet away. She looked to see where they led, but she had a feeling she already knew.

The beach.

She ran down the slope and saw two sets of tracks in the wet sand. One was a set of footprints. Small ones. The others were smaller still, but not a child's. Each print was made up of four small lines, like bird's feet. They were all around Jack's and so was the blood.

Sarah followed them towards the South rocks and then it hit her. Eric. That name—that god damn name. The day Jack found those crabs he'd said Eric told him where to find them. Oh God, she realised, it must have come from this place.

And now she'd delivered her son back to its lair.

She wiped the mist from her eyes as she climbed over the rocks. The tide had left them slick. More than once her feet slipped on the smooth surface and she fell. The wind was freezing and her clothes were already soaked by the time she reached the mouth of the cave. The entrance was dark. It loomed over, threatening to swallow her. She didn't want to go in alone.

Looking around for help, all along the beach and the town above it were empty. There was no one that could help her, no one to call upon. She was alone. More than that though, at that precise moment she felt like the only person left in the world. But this wasn't her world anymore; it was some parallel nightmare where creatures from dark recesses could come to take the only thing she had left to love. He's just a boy, she thought, I brought him out here to be happy. Today's his birthday, for Christ's sake. If I'd had the bottle to tell him about Kieran in the first place, we might not have even come here.

It's all my fault.

Sarah doubled over as her stomach creased in agony. That cold black ocean in her gut rushed up her throat and spewed out onto the rocks. The pain it brought was emotional as well as physical, as now the cold was gone she felt nothing left inside her. She was hollow. Empty.

That feeling, she realised, was how every moment would feel from then on if she didn't find Jack here today.

She had to find him. There was no other choice.

She took her keys out of her pocket and unhooked the small torch she used to find locks in the dark and started towards the cave entrance. As she neared the entrance though, something in the corner of her eye stopped her. One of Jack's trainers was bobbing in the sea close to the rocks. She rushed over and managed to pull it out before it drifted out of reach. There were tear marks on one side. His other shoe was floating further out, drifting around the side of the cliff face.

Without hesitating, Sarah climbed down into the sea and waded towards it. Her heart palpitated as the frigid grey water reached up to her chest. Past his other shoe was his t-shirt. Then, with the keyring torch in her mouth to keep it dry, she swam around the side of the cliffs, where Jack's trousers floated out from the mouth of another cave. Much smaller than the main one, almost unnoticeable thanks to the warped tree roots that hung down from the cliff and covered the entrance, she would have missed it if not for her son's clothes. She wondered how many people actually knew about this one.

The first thing Sarah noticed as she climbed out of the water onto a shelf of damp rock was how quiet this smaller cave was. The sea, though only feet away, sounded so distant. Only a hollow warbling resounded through the narrow chamber. It was warm in there too. Humid. But still she shivered.

Within a few feet the cave became total darkness. The rocks around her were sharp, with limestone stalactites and stalagmites jutting from the ceiling and the walls. She used the torch sparingly as she crawled on her hands and knees, navigating mostly by touch, then as the cave narrowed had to lie on her front and shuffle inch by inch. She became stuck more than once, but with enough effort managed to wriggle through. Her heart pounded from fear. By the time the cave widened, her arms and legs were covered with cuts, and blood flowed freely from her shoulder.

Hot air, stinking of salt and fish, came from the cave ahead, billowing out towards her in slow, breath-like increments. But soon she heard another sound. One that was closer, familiar: A child's whimpering. Then something

else followed it. Another voice she recognised, but this time in a relaxed tone that made her shudder.

"Skuuudaaa. Ahh, skuuudaaa."

Piercing the darkness were two white ovals, bright against the blackness of the cave, but a faded, milky white with red veins around the edges. The eyes closed, their slits operating sideways as it made that sound again.

Sarah shone the torch while it wasn't looking. Her next breath got caught in her chest as at last she beheld Eric. It was small, about the size of a dog, with a disproportionately large head. It sat down on its haunches. All four bony limbs were covered in barbs that swayed back and forth with its breathing. She wondered why it hadn't heard her crawling through the cave, but then she realised.

It was preoccupied.

Her son lay flat on the rock floor beside it. His eyes were open, but rolled back. A grimace of pain crossed his semi-lucid face.

Sarah felt something new come to life in her stomach. Not cold, but hot. Boiling. It replaced that black, bottomless ocean and she felt its warmth spread and imbue her with purpose. The pain from her cuts was forgotten and she edged towards the creature, hoping to sneak up behind it. Her son murmured in pain. Sarah saw then that a long appendage, as black as the rest of it, extended from Eric's torso and it had punctured the bare skin of Jack's stomach. The creature groaned and let out another of its phrases as the proboscis bulged. Something emerged from the creature's torso and travelled along the fleshy tube. The swelling reached Jack and her son mewled as the puncture wound in his stomach stretched. The object pumped inside him.

Then another swelling began travelling down the appendage, followed by another.

Was this why had it followed him for months on end? Was this its endgame all along? Since that day on the beach, was this always going to happen?

At that point Sarah didn't care why. The second she heard her son's cries, everything else ceased to exist. She felt around the low-ceilinged cave for a loose rock, but as she picked one up her shoe slipped on the damp surface and the rock clanged to the ground. The creature turned. Its eyes grew wide, then narrowed as they focused on her. Sarah dashed towards it, shining her torch in the thing's eyes, not giving it time to use its quickness to escape. It reeled back from the light and Sarah grabbed hold of its throat. It shrieked like scraping metal as Sarah pulled its proboscis out of her son. Blood spat from the puncture wound.

The Skudda lashed out with its bony arms and legs. The spines along its limbs cut a large gash across Sarah's shoulder and stomach. Her blood flowed, but she didn't stop. The creature's struggles were cut short as Sarah pulled on its appendage and it convulsed in pain. The organ was meaty and tough, slickened with secretions like raw meat. She wrapped it around her hand like a rope and pulled until the muscles tore and the proboscis ripped off. Her hand was washed in hot blood.

The scream the creature made then was indescribable. Sarah knew nothing like it. To stop it, she grabbed the creature's head and twisted until she felt the neck bones grind and break apart.

The Skudda fell limp in her hands, but Sarah wasn't done. Jack was all she had left. The only thing that mattered. He was her world and she was his. She couldn't lose him to this thing. It wasn't enough to just kill it. It had to be destroyed. She remembered her promise.

Like a wild animal, Sarah dug her fingernails into the creature's wiry neck. Its skin was tough and wet, but she managed to puncture it. Once the wound was open she shoved her fingers inside and broke its brittle vertebrae apart, but her lust for revenge was still not sated. She cried and panted and screamed in frenzy, not stopping until its head was completely detached. So focused was Sarah on eradicating this creature that she never noticed the sighs of sepulchral air around her were getting louder.

Blood and tears flowed from her as the headless body dropped to the floor. She darted over to her son. Upon seeing her boy's stricken face, the rage that had driven her suddenly lifted. She came to her senses and examined him. His breaths were shallow, but he was alive. The blood from his stomach was a steady trickle, but the skin bulged where something lay beneath the surface. Sarah hesitated. She knew how to end his suffering, but it would mean causing more pain.

With the torch held between her teeth, she saw that clogging the puncture wound was a murky, blackish-green mass. Gelatinous to touch, in the torch light she could see it was full of translucent liquid with a tiny black shape in its centre. Sarah almost threw up. The black shape was a foetus. The object in her son was an egg.

Her fingers kept slipping from the blood covering them as she worked to gently squeeze the egg out from underneath like a cyst. The first one popped out without rupturing and even though he was paralyzed, Jack's face twisted. Sarah put her hand on his forehead to calm him down as she worked her other fingers beneath his skin to get the next egg out.

There were five inside him.

She crushed them all with her shoe, then took her t-shirt off, rung the sea water out of it and pressed it over the date-sized hole in Jack's stomach to quell the bleeding. Then she dragged him toward the tunnel she'd entered from.

It was then that she heard it: That ancient breath reeking of salt and dead fish. Beneath the chamber came a slimy, whirling noise. She hurried as the sound grew. Before she left the chamber she shone her torch and saw the Skudda's carcass and head being dragged through a tiny gap in the limestone at the far side of the cave. Something was down there, below in the further depths. Sarah felt the presence of something much larger. Ancient. Had she killed its offspring? She didn't care. It tried to take hers. It deserved to die.

That ancient breath sounded again, only this time it growled.

She was close to the entrance now. The sound of the waves lapping against the rock shelf was just ahead. Sarah hurried out of the cave and swam, carrying her son, all she had left, over to the rocks by the South Beach. She could no longer hear the rumblings from the cave now and the tide was further out. The sea mist had cleared and she spied a few early morning joggers on the beach.

Back on the sand, the adrenaline left her and she began to feel the wounds on her shoulder and stomach. She smelled the creature's blood on her. Then her strength failed as she collapsed to her knees and dropped Jack on the beach. She shivered, barely clothed. Now she had time to process it, her mind was unable to comprehend the things she'd witnessed, the things she now knew were real. She felt her grasp on reality begin to slip. Everything became distant, muted as the beach before her began to fade.

Before it all went dark she saw a middle-aged man in fluorescent running shorts approaching.

Sarah woke up in the hospital four days later. She took up smoking a few days after that. Detective Inspector Bloch said it would help with the stress, so long as she didn't get addicted, but after what she'd witnessed, she never even tried to quit.

"Raving. That was the word the old man used. He said you were raving about some cave when he found you. Then you blacked out." DI Bloch raised an eyebrow. Jack lay stabilised in the ICU further down the ward. Despite her insisting, Sarah wasn't allowed to see him just yet. Her wounds had been sewn and bandaged and between them they were given vaccinations for just about everything. When she was fully conscious, the police asked to speak to her in private.

Sarah told them the truth. Full disclosure. And the second she'd finished talking she realised just how much of a mistake that was. She had nothing to show for it. The eggs were destroyed and the Skudda's carcass had been taken. All evidence to show she wasn't insane was gone. As soon as she'd mentioned her husband's death, she knew they'd write her up as just some grieving mother gone mad. Even she had trouble believing some of the details as she recited them. Before the interview was over the police were already talking about Social Services. Bloch outright told her she might never see her son again.

As soon as she was discharged, Bloch placed her in handcuffs and escorted her to his car. She spent that night and a few more after in a cell. Social Services didn't take long to decide either, given her testimony and history. Her appeals were quickly declined.

Every year from then, whenever she posted Jack a letter, Christmas card, or a birthday card, never knowing if he'd actually see them, but always hoping, she reminded herself that she had saved his life. For all her failings, she'd managed this one thing. She'd kept her promise. Whatever story people told Jack about his mother's mental breakdown didn't matter. Whatever Jack did with his life then was because of her. She'd ventured into the very mouth of Hell and pulled him out. Her absence was a small sacrifice for his life, and she paid it gladly.

But every night from then until the day that old age claimed her, she'd lie awake, hearing the screams of the Skudda in her mind and reciting one terrible, unshakable thought: children all over the world have imaginary friends...

THE END

```
ABOUT THE AUTHOR
Sam Graham proudly hails from
Hull, East Yorkshire. When not
writing he plays the guitar,
hikes and drinks copious amounts
of tea. He's loved horror ever
since he was 10 and first saw
Palmer's head rip open in The
Thing. Nowadays he collects cult
horror films and enjoys subject-
ing his partner to films like
Slugs and Society for a laugh. In
2017 his speculative novella, The
Iron Country won 1st in NAWG's
novella competition and is cur-
rently with a publisher. His fa-
vourite writers are Moorcock,
Robert E. Howard, Hemingway and
of course, H.P. Lovecraft.
```

THE DEMONS OF KURSK by James McLachlan

There was a deafening noise, the hollow reverberating sound of dying metal. Then it all had to fight with a great ringing in the ears, and there was suddenly a terrible heat and the overwhelming feeling of urgency. I was shaking Borislav, but he was no longer there, only a dead lump, nothing but an impediment. I was pushing, pushing with my hands and then with my whole body, forcing my way through, hammering on metal, desperate. Finally the hatch burst open and there was an explosion of flame and cold air. But I dared not stop. Pushing my way through the burning metal hatch, with the smell of cordite and the muffled sound of distant explosions, my coat was corking me in the opening, and I was burning. Then with great pain I was somehow through, then falling, my coat snagging the guide horns of the spare track links, and I hung for a time before falling to the ground into a slush of snow and mud and oil. My senses were numbed, but for the rawness of my flesh, my exhaustion, and the irresistible urgency to move. I needed to get away from the burning tank.

Groggily I got to my knees. My ears were still ringing madly, but I could see the huge plumes of dirt that were being blown into the air from the shells that had failed to hit home, covering the sky in what looked like smudges of brown charcoal. I crawled for the first few metres until I managed to get up on my feet, but there was nowhere to go, the terrain was flat and exposed. My body ached. I knew I was already dead, so why prolong the inevitable?

There was a little explosion of snow just before me. I looked up and saw tanks everywhere, our T-34s and a lot of the Fritzie's new Panthers. I spotted the one my crew had been firing on before we ourselves were hit. It seemed we had got them after all—or someone had. It too was on fire, and one of its tracks had been blown off. It looked dead. A Fritzie was jogging towards me from that direction with a bloodstained coat sleeve. He halted and took aim at me with his rifle. I started to run, but there was nowhere to go. Another bullet barely missed me, thwacking into the snow and mud about a metre to my right. Then I saw I was approaching the edge of what appeared to be a cliff, or at least some sort of drop, which had been hard to distinguish from the surrounding terrain until I drew near it, so I ran towards that.

The seconds that followed were some of the longest I have ever known, expecting at any moment to feel the searing kiss of a bullet as it thudded into my back. I thought my lungs were going to burst as I reached the edge of what turned out to be a steep descent down a hillside torn open like a wound by heavy shelling. I looked back to the Fritzie; he was still making straight for me, and now seemed to be shouting something. Again he stopped to take aim at me. At this range it seemed impossible he could miss, which left me with only one option. I stumbled forward and flung myself at the edge, landing just short of it, then kicking myself over I was tumbling and falling down the steep slope through the freezing snow and gravel. The burns on my neck and face were torn and gouged as I slid, causing me to cry out, but my voice was drowned in a barrage of fire from our nearby anti-tank guns. Again and again I tried to grip on to something, but there was nothing but hard, loose rubble all the way down. An object appeared in my periphery, but amid the confusion and terror of my uncontrolled momentum, it was impossible to tell in which direction it lay.

Then suddenly I had stopped. All was dark and silent, and then the world slowly faded back into view. My head was wedged against something very hard and hurt dreadfully; it was difficult to believe I had been wearing my padded tanker helmet at all. Had I not I think I would have been killed. Everything about me hurt and all I wanted to do was lie there, untroubled by any great awareness. But I dared not stay, exposed on the side of that hill, and soon the sound of shelling was once more roaring about me, vibrating through the ground into my skull until I thought it would burst. My eyes opened and a terrible dull light shot in, burning my brain out like an incendiary.

At some point I was able to lift my head and I began to look around me. I had come to rest against a large chunk of virgin rock blown from out of the hillside, along with other bits of rubble now covered with snow. Blood from a wound in my head started to run into my eyes, causing my vision to blur, so I gingerly wiped it away with the back of my hand, reminding me of winter mornings from my childhood. I then noticed a small opening in the crater of blasted rock that looked large enough for me to shelter in, so I began to slowly crawl and drag myself towards it. A pain in my leg told me I had probably been injured there as well, but I didn't stop to examine it. I think I assumed I was about to die anyway.

As I crawled into the crevice, I found the remains of an exploded 76.2 mm shell—one of ours. There was an opening into the hillside here, big enough that I was able to fit my head inside and found it continued for some way underground, ending in darkness. It must have been blasted open when that shell exploded. In my exhausted state it took several minutes of physical work to widen the opening enough for me to crawl into, luckily the surrounding rock was cracked in several places. But I was no sooner in than I found the way barred by a solid mass of immovable rock, which would have required explosives to shift. However, there was a gap running underneath this, through which I could see that the cavity continued, so by digging out the loose gravel and small rocks with my hands, I was able to get past. Here I could finally let myself rest, feeling relatively safe from the fighting that was going on outside.

If anything it was even colder in here and my leg was paining me again. I felt it and found I had been shot, but the bullet had apparently only grazed me,

ripping at the leg of my overalls and some of the flesh underneath. It was too dark to see very well, but after feeling about me I discovered I was in an open space almost large enough to stand up in, and that it continued further on into the hill. I remembered I had some matches with me so I struck a light. I now saw it was not so much a single tunnel as one of a network of faults and fissures working their way through the rock and forming what must be a maze of narrow passageways. A few metres down a sloping path into this confusion the ceiling shot up about ten metres, becoming a great black rock sky over my head at the very edge of the match light.

Suddenly I heard a noise behind me, echoing through the recently excavated cavity from the entrance. Someone else was crawling into the cave. But how could they? The entrance was in an inaccessible place halfway down the side of a steep slope; I had only found it myself through chance. Someone must have seen me going in. I thought of the Fritzie who had been running and shooting at me, and had caused me to jump off the side of the hill in the first place. This did not bode well; I would be trapped in here.

My match went out and darkness returned. I moved further into the cave, my fingers quickly running over every surface, feeling my way around the twists and turns and dead-ends of the close rock pathways. But I had no idea where I was going. What if I ended up blundering into whoever it was I was trying to get away from? I could go no further without being able to see. I took my hands from the walls, knelt down, and began straining to listen for even the slightest sound. All was perfectly quiet; the only thing I could hear was my own pulse throbbing in my ears as it pumped blood and adrenaline through my head, making me dizzy.

A light appeared. At first it was just the merest glimmer and was apt to disappear, challenging, almost tormenting my senses. Then it became a dull but definite presence, constantly with me, but unwilling to reveal the direction of its source. It grew stronger. I held my breath and dared not move, whoever it was that commanded that light was able to see by it, but I could not. Closer and closer it came, brighter and brighter; hesitant, but steady. The sound of boot steps scraping on stone could now be heard as someone descended on me from behind the light, and then suddenly stopped. The nerve-shattering near misses I had suffered at the ever-grasping hands of Death's messengers had counted for nothing, it seemed, nothing but to be a torment to my final and inevitable demise. They had found me; all of them: Fate, Death, and whoever now stood before me in the flesh. I was too frightened to move, the light exploding in my vision as if the world had been set alight, paralysing me against the rock to which I now clung. My sense of touch, for so long the only reliable indicator of what existed outside of my body, would not allow me to break my hold of this only physical certainty, my sight now merely blanketed yellow instead of black.

There came a voice. But could I still trust my sense of hearing, distorted by the echoes and refractions of this terrible place? It was harsh and strained, like the whisper of a starving man, a man out of patience. But also perhaps one far past all things, so far past that there was no longer any reason to stand, or breathe, or think, or even to have

been born at all. The only explanation—for in truth it could hardly be called a reason—as to why he had not dropped down dead upon finding me, was because the time for that had long since passed him by. He carried on because he didn't know what else he was supposed to do. The one thing more intolerable than what was happening to him was for him to remain inactive while it was going on. He had been seized by it, assimilated, and carried along in its mad stampede.

I could not understand what he said because I don't speak German. That he was speaking German was all I needed to know. He repeated himself and moved the light so it was not shining directly into my eyes. After a few moments I was able to make him out, silhouetted against the rock: his coat, his helmet, and above all his rifle, pointed directly at me. He held a torch with the fingers of his left hand as it cradled the stock. I was still unable to raise my arms, but there seemed little point in the gesture, as what could I possibly do to attack him? He spoke again, more purposeful this time, with more anger, and the weapon shook in his hands.

I began to slowly get to my feet, as I presumed that was what he wanted. My eyes had adjusted somewhat better to the presence of the light by now, and I was able to make out some of his features. He looked terrible, possibly even worse than I presume I looked myself. His uniform was torn, bloodstained and burnt, there were burns to his hands and the right cheek of his face, and his hair hung drenched with oily sweat from beneath his helmet. As I have said, he seemed to be the Fritzie who had been shooting at me, but it was hard to tell, everyone looked the same by this stage in the fighting: thin, unshaven, and covered in mud. I only knew who my friends were because they were wearing roughly the same uniform as myself.

He spat me some more incomprehensible gibberish, although it obviously meant enough to him to bother saying it to me when he must have known I couldn't understand. Then having said his piece, he made to shoot me. I remember thinking there was a lot to recommend a quick death just then: the cold, the mud, the noise, the starvation, the blood and the filth... the iron fist of Stalin and the Party back home. But I was not being given much of a choice. I could go nowhere, I had no weapon; I could not even speak German.

Then it happened. From the darkness behind the Fritzie there sprang two or three root-like strands, each about the size of a thick piece of rope, which dextrously wrapped themselves around his legs and began pulling him backwards. As he uttered a cry of surprise, the unexpected jolt toppled him to the ground, though he managed to hold onto his rifle and torch, the beam of light flashing and streaking in every direction as he began struggling against the tethers now trying to drag him around a corner. Then the light went out, and immediately his cry, which he had kept up in one form or another all the time he was being hauled away, turned to a scream—one I shall never forget. In a few moments it lessened to a series of rapid little babbling gasps of surprise and incomprehension, as if the man's fright was now only of secondary importance to something else. That too ceased, and after the last of the reverberations had dissipated through the tunnels and fissures in the rock, there was no sound at all, and I was alone in the dark once more.

Except I knew this was not so. Somewhere there was a German soldier —alive or dead—and somewhere near him there was whatever it was that had taken him. I had no idea what to do, yet again my senses were reduced to that of touch and sound. Feeling was of no use to me until it was too late, and I could hear nothing. I could see no real change in my circumstances; I was lost in this dark earthen tomb and the likelihood of my stumbling about for a while until I found a way out was simply too absurd to be contemplated seriously. But even so, I would have to do it, and before those tentacle-like things found me. Suddenly the thought of going up against thousands of heavily armed Germans with only a few hours training and with no radio in my tank wasn't as bad as it had once seemed.

I remained crouching there for what seemed a very long time, but I have no way of telling how long it really was. I was paralysed by fear, indecision, and hopelessness, until I even became frightened by the fact that I wasn't doing anything. Finally I struck a match. It flared and spluttered in the damp air, died down, and then grew into a steady flame. As it lighted the walls about me, my eyes scanned for a passage to follow, preferably in the opposite direction to which the Fritzie had been taken.

Slowly I crept, little by little, desperately trying not to make any noise. After a while I halted, as I thought I saw a slight movement in front of me, a change in the shadows cast by my light. A few moments more and I spotted the Fritzie standing, or leaning, against the rock. He had gone deathly white in the face, even though it was stained with dried blood and dirt. He had no expression, showed no sign of what he was feeling, but his eyes stared out, unblinking, in the most appalling manner, as if his soul had departed his body, leaving the windows flung wide open after it. Entwined around his body there writhed a mass of the black tentacle-like appendages, preventing him from moving, whilst still more were worming their way over the rock around him, as if sensing out the environment.

My match went out and I hurriedly lit another. I then saw, and with terrible realisation instantly understood the meaning of, two large oval-shaped glints reflecting back at me from the rock just behind the Fritzie. Their shape, and particularly their size, I had never seen before, but they were undoubtedly two huge shiny black eyes.

Immediately a shapeless mass came to life, as if it had emerged from out of the very rock, and sent out its repulsive tentacles to ensnare me as well, for I now understood they were connected to it. Its body, if that is what it should be called, was jet black with a slight sheen to it, a bit like the leathery casing of a shark's egg. There were no holes or orifices that I could detect; its eyes (if they were eyes), rather than being two jelly-like balls sitting inside bone sockets, seemed to be an integrated part of the thing's hide. From underneath and all around the lower portion of the body (which had no describable shape, rather it seemed to change shape with its every movement) there sprang the innumerable rope-like tentacles or feelers.

All this I saw in the space of a few seconds, before I too felt the cold explorative touch of those black fingers tapping their way over my coat, and I dropped the match. Plunged back into darkness, I have no visual reference for what happened from this point onward, only sounds and what I could feel. Terrifying beyond description, the tentacles started to wrap themselves around me, and then began feeling their way over the exposed areas of my skin. They were cold and rubbery, twitching with nervous life, entwining me like coils of rope. I was unable to move; the strength of their grip was as if the rock above were pushing down on me with the pressure of an alien atmosphere. I could do nothing against it.

After what seemed an age, I felt a tension being exerted on the tentacles, and there came a horrible wet gravelly sort of sound, as though something were being dragged towards me. I tried not to think of it, to push all images from my mind, but there it remained all the same: the leathery carcass of the creature sliding towards me, its many mooring lines anchored ahead of it, and presumably bringing the German along.

Then the tension slackened and I could hear a high pitched humming sound coming from somewhere, which grew steadily in volume until it became a piercing agony, throbbing right into my head. I desperately wanted to block it out, to clap my hands over my ears, and once more I struggled to break free from my terrible bindings, but it was impossible. The ringing swiftly died down, however, until there was utter silence. But although the noise had gone, something remained for all that. There was a presence, some sort of trace residue, its only physical manifestation a sensation that enveloped my head, blocking out even the ambience of the cave, so in my mind the new silence was almost overwhelming.

Into this there broke a voice that sounded like a roar in my present state, but was probably no more than a whisper. It was so terrifyingly near to me that I was unable to comprehend how it was possible for any physical separation to exist between myself and it. Surely it must be some part of myself that I could hear, speaking with its own personality and voice. But then, no, not a voice, not really, it was not speech such as I had ever encountered it, it was more of an impression, an idea only. It came directly into my head, dry and untouched by the ether around me, a direct link of thought between myself and... I was overtaken by a violent unthinking urge to claw the presence from my mind, and I believe I would have attempted to rip it from my actual skull if I had been able to. But I could not move.

It was the tentacled black shape talking to me, whispering its alien thoughts right into my mind. That it should actually want to communicate with humanity! How was I to reconcile this with a lifetime of nightmares and sleepless fear of things in the dark? It was as if some of the 'prime' had been removed from this primal being, making it so much more than a mere bestial killer and devourer of men, which all my instincts told me it must be. There was now great intelligence behind its horror; like a sane maniac it was capable of remaining undetected for longer, allowing it more opportunity to strike. I could not escape it through any physical means, for our minds were now interlocked, and I felt it wanting to control my thinking.

Then there came clarity. I suddenly felt very relaxed and open to what I was hearing. It wanted to know why the German had been chasing me, and why he intended to kill me. I had forgotten about my friend just then, I think I had assumed he was dead, and had been ever since the light had been extinguished. Nor had I for a moment regarded him as being a part of my connection to the creature, but it was now obvious that we were linked in a sort of mental triangle, and everything I heard, he heard also. All this flashed through my mind in the space of a few moments, and I knew it all to be true.

The German himself gave no response to the question, but I presume like myself he had been stunned and stupefied by the sudden intrusion of the alien will now probing at his mind. And whereas I had been afforded a mental respite in which to recover, and was in fact only now awakening to the reality that perhaps not all the horrors I had imagined were about to come true, he had not, and was presumably still struggling to make sense of it all.

I believe I was correct in this assumption, as despite his hesitation, he did answer, although he appeared not to have grasped the mechanism by which the creature was communicating with us, because he answered by speaking aloud in his own language. All the same, I was able to understand him, and I thought his explanation quite elegant in its simplicity. He said my tank crew had killed his, so he wanted me dead. I had expected his thinking to be more along the lines of the fact that killing each other was the reason we were here, for I was as guilty of this as he. It was true I had not been chasing anyone through this cave—although I had no gun or grenade with which to do so—but up on the surface we were all as one. I had been trying to kill, and I had killed, machine-gunning the enemy whether they were a threat to me personally or not. This was how I assumed the German was going to frame his answer, but I don't think he cared about his own moral motivations just then; I represented what was wrong here, and damn everything else. Maybe it was because my mind had been prised so far open, but I was filled with the horror of my own justifications as I had never been before. I would never know how many men and tanks I had helped to destroy, I felt as if I were the destroyer of the whole world.

Through images and notions placed in our minds, the creature showed us what it was: an ancient rock-dweller, living deep down in the earth, in a sort of semi-dormancy. It had felt the vibrations from the shelling and explosions going on far above, and had awoke with curiosity. Its great ever-sensing tentacles reached out to find a way through the cracks and openings in the rock to the commotion and activity of the surface, its body sliding and bumping along behind them.

It listened to what the German had to say, and then wanted to know why my people were killing his in the first place. I tried to explain why we were fighting, that there were two groups of men, one trying to invade the lands of the other and wanting to take control and make slaves of us. I told it that thousands of my people were starving.

It remained silent for a time after this, as if it was thinking, and I felt its presence leave my mind. Then it broke through once more and spoke to both of us. In light of our mutual warring it wished to determine which of our two sides had the greatest moral right to win

out. Or to put it another way, which of us was the least guilty of disturbing it. We were each to present it with our reasons and excuses; the loser to be... and I shuddered as the thought appeared in my mind... the loser was to be devoured. In an attempt to spare the reader some of the horror of that moment, I have chosen this one word to translate what we were told in detail. From my unique perspective, plugged directly into our captor's mind, I was left in no doubt that it was promising to literally eat us. The winner would be allowed to go free. Although I cannot say how much of a victory the creature thought this was to be, as it clearly meant going back to all the dangers of the battle. I wonder if in its alien mind it saw this as a just, and ironic, punishment also.

The Fritzie got in first here. Unsurprisingly, he would have the creature believe Germany had no choice but to invade, that they were being pre-emptive against the threat of Russian bolshevism, they were struggling to defend their culture. In fact their very existence was at stake—the battle between races and all the usual sentiment.

I could not have this, and pointed out that Germany merely wanted our resources, our oil and iron ore. In fact they needed more oil to continue their march across Europe and to conquer Britain. The Nazis regarded them, us, and most everyone else as sub-human. Fritzie didn't bother to refute this, but attempted to sweeten it by saying they didn't want the whole country, they just wanted to annex part of Ukraine to populate with German farmers. As 'superior Aryans' they were entitled to the land for their people to live. If they could capture Leningrad and Moscow they would negotiate a peaceful surrender for Russia.

Naturally I disagreed again, and soon the justifications and rebuttals were coming thick and fast, backwards and forwards, so that I find it hard to recall exactly what was said with any degree of accuracy. But for the Red Army, and indeed most of the Russian people, it was a war of patriotism. We fought for our beloved country, our honour, and for our liberty. Ours was a just cause, given we had been invaded; Stalin himself called it a "Patriotic War ... of the entire Soviet people". The Fritzie was equally adamant on his own side— who knows, maybe he even believed it— and neither of us was willing to admit to anything less than the most glowing of moral intentions. It seemed we had reached an impasse, and I wondered what the creature was making of it all. Looking back, if I were it, I think I would have been tempted to damn us both; we two representatives of the human race must have looked a pathetic and degraded sight. But in the heat of the argument neither of us was concerned with that.

Things then changed overwhelmingly for the better, and I forgot all about the pitiful impression we must have been making of ourselves. For it turned out that the monster had only been amusing itself at our expense. Its kind, it intimated—and I shuddered at the thought of more of these loathsome creatures—were not permitted to kill other, less civilised and evolved beings. It was never going to eat either of us. And for that I could forgive the 'lesser evolved' slur.

The relief I felt at being told this is hard to put into words, especially as it came while I was struggling to express myself in terms of thoughts and impressions so the thing would understand. Perhaps I can convey something of it by the way the Fritzie greeted this new development. He appeared to take it on board and recover his composure quite quickly, as after a few moments he mumbled something in real speech, which I could not understand, and then suddenly set upon me, bursting from the blind darkness like an arc of electricity. At first I assumed it must be the thing, having decided to crush out our lives after all, but in fact it had loosened its grip on me, and had done so during its confession that it couldn't devour us; I had simply failed to notice it. Instead, a pair of human hands flailed around until they found my throat, and locking around it, began throttling the life out of me. With the suddenness of this double reversal of fortune and my nerves weakened through the prolonged tension under which they had been held, I began to succumb to the attack very quickly, and I knew it was the end.

I was just falling into unconsciousness when I heard what sounded like the monster speaking once more. It said it had been testing us yet again, and I remember thinking something about the horrible intrusion it was making in our lives by doing all this. What did it really want with us? I was further infuriated by the almost conversational way in which it had spoken; surely a revelation such as that deserved a more serious tone. It said it had been playing with us, testing us, and that we had failed. Or was it that only one of us had failed? There was a scream, and then possibly another, but mixed with a muffled dry crunching sound, and there I must have fallen senseless.

When I came to myself, something which I considered almost miraculous, both the monster and the German were gone. After feeling around for a time I found the man's torch and managed to get it working. Of the rifle there was no sign, nor was there anything which might indicate that I had not been completely alone for all the time I had spent in the caves. I did find a dark rusty discolouration about where I thought the German had been standing during my last moments of consciousness, but I dared not examine it too closely. I wanted to leave, as I thought I would be safer above ground during a tank battle than in that cave. With the aid of the torch I did manage to somehow find my way out and to rejoin the fighting, where I eventually ended up at a field hospital—if a couple of tents in the snow can be called such a thing. I have been told that I mentioned my strange experience while I lay recovering, but of course I was not taken seriously. My tales of monsters in the dark were put down to the delusions of a shocked mind.

Somehow I survived the war, and never spoke again of what happened to me that day in October 1943 during the Battle of Kursk. How could I? Hundreds of thousands would die in one way or another, with all the related horrors that mass death brings, but the world didn't need to know about this one. And neither did I, for I really had no way of telling if I had not simply been suffering from delusions after all. There may never have been any tentacle horror from under the earth, disturbed by our terrible warring. Maybe it was my own troubled mind reacting to all the

deep dark things that can lie beneath the surface.

Frankly, I wish never to find out.

THE END

ABOUT THE AUTHOR

James McLachlan is one of Australia's most acclaimed writers of dark and humorous fiction. Or he would be, he just can't be bothered being famous. He is the author of *The Satanist, A Black Metal Ghost Story*, and other novels.

THE ANCIENT TRACKERS by John H Dromey

Wayne Stratton and Susan Morton considered themselves extremely lucky. Convincing their history professor to go on a field trip with them had been a hard sell for a couple of reasons.

In the first place, Professor Gates actively discouraged any of his students from pursuing the study of vanished civilizations which had not left incontrovertibly identifiable living descendants.

The discovery of a Viking coin in North America would excite the prof's academic interest only if he could exploit the significance of the numismatic find in conjunction with a DNA study of modern-day Scandinavians. Lost Mayan cities? Maybe. Anasazi artefacts? Don't hold your breath.

Secondly, as a practical matter, it seemed likely that even gently rolling hills would present a serious challenge to the professor's hiking skills. That conclusion could be drawn from his total lack of athleticism. He only explored the upper halls of academe if they were accessible by elevator.

Dean Wirth

Professor Gates was not the outdoor type. His pale complexion prompted some students to speculate that exposure to direct sunlight might cause him to spontaneously combust. If any had dared to say that out loud in his presence, the professor most likely would have chided the speaker for splitting an infinitive and taken no further action. Verbal gymnastics were apparently all the exercise he required.

The hidebound instructor was compelled to make an exception to his criteria for research projects when unseasonably heavy spring rains unearthed countless long-buried stones within easy driving distance of the university. Many of those stones were covered with ancient markings.

For this unprecedented outing with a couple of his star pupils, Professor Gates leaned heavily on a wooden staff and walked with a stoop. At one point the two graduate students had outstripped their faculty advisor by nearly a quarter of a mile despite their bulging backpacks laden with digging tools and rock hammers. The gap had narrowed somewhat in the last half hour when the students were obliged to slow their pace considerably as the ascent became increasingly steep and the footing more and more uneven.

Breathing heavily, the two young people sat on a rock outcrop.

"I'm beginning to think this expedition was a bad idea," Susan said.

"It's a bit late to have second thoughts."

"I know, Wayne, but I can't help myself. Professor Gates is creepy."

"I'll admit he speaks in stilted English and dresses like someone out of a Victorian novel, but other than that, what's not to like?"

"I'm serious, Wayne. Two nights ago, I was in the library reading a book that's on reserve when I happened to glance up. I caught the professor looking my way. It was almost as though he were studying me. It freaked me out."

"On the remote chance no one's told you lately, Suze, you're rather easy on the eyes."

"Thanks for the compliment, but he wasn't giving me that kind of look. Later that night I had the sensation that I was being followed. I felt someone was lurking in the shadows outside the dorm."

"Do you think it was the professor?"

"I don't know," Susan said.

"Well, he's most definitely following both of us today."

"Yeah, but it's different in broad daylight. I just hope we get back to the campus before dark. With that in mind, maybe we should get a move on."

"Let's wait just a little longer," Wayne said. "The air is thin here."

"Tell me something I don't know," Susan responded.

"Maybe I will."

Wayne pulled an envelope out of his shirt pocket and extracted several sheets of paper.

"What's that?" Susan asked.

"I sent an inquiry about ancient languages to a professor emeritus of Ol' Misky U. He's reputed to have had full access to the library's closed stacks. This is his response. It came this morning and I haven't had time to decipher his handwriting yet. On the other hand, his drawings of old petroglyphs are remarkably detailed and should prove very useful when we write our research paper."

"Why didn't you email him? He could have scanned the drawings."

"No, he couldn't. Dr. Foster is an electronic recluse. He doesn't even have a telephone. I was lucky to find his address in an old college catalogue."

"Just how bad is his penmanship?" Susan asked.

"See for yourself." Wayne handed her the letter.

"It's bad, but I've seen worse. I worked in a pharmacy for a couple of summers when I was in high school."

"You can understand those scribbles?"

"Yes," she said, turning a page. "I can make out most of the words anyway."

Wayne shrugged his shoulders. "Well, that information will keep for right now. Although it might be nice to know exactly what the runes and hieroglyphs on the guide stones mean, surely the fact we're finding the trail markers closer and closer together means we're getting near the site we're seeking. We should know very soon now whether it's a burial ground, or a place of some other ritual importance. Either way, the track is clearly marked, so we're obviously intended to follow it."

Wayne stopped to catch his breath.

"Maybe not," Susan said, as she continued to read the letter.

"Don't keep me in suspense, Suze. We both have a lot riding on this project."

"You're telling me?"

"Yes, I am. Our stick-to-the-campus professor was reluctant to give his approval. He grilled me at length about my ancestry before agreeing to this excursion. It may not be obvious from my surname, but some branches of my family have lived around here for a very long time."

"Mine too."

"Do you think that fact may have influenced his decision?" Wayne asked.

"It could have."

"Since our semester grades are at stake, Suze, maybe you should tell me what you've learned from the letter."

"According to Dr. Foster the symbols on the markers we found are warning signs indicating 'keep out' or 'turn back.'"

"Are you kidding me?"

"I'm afraid not." Susan used her finger to trace a design in the dust. "We're to be especially on the lookout for this squiggle."

"I've already seen it. That particular rune was engraved on the archway of stones we passed through a short while ago," Wayne said. "What does it mean?"

"The point of no return."

"From where?"

"Dr. Foster doesn't say."

Susan started hyperventilating.

"Calm down," Wayne said. "The thin air can be attributed to a change in altitude. It's hardly an indication that we've passed through an ancient portal into an alternate dimension or anything creepy like that."

"No animals," Susan gasped.

"You're right, of course, but that doesn't necessarily mean something sinister is going on. What kind of animals did you expect to see in the high country anyway? Mountain goats? They aren't indigenous to this part of the country. It's true I haven't seen a rabbit for quite some time today, but I haven't seen a lettuce patch either. We're in a barren spot. Thin air and a lack of vegetation could cause bunnies and field mice to stay away from here, and without an abundant food supply birds of prey would also keep their distance. To relieve your anxiety, though, I'll check the GPS on my cell phone."

A short while later, Wayne said, "No signal. We must be in a dead zone."

"Something's wrong with our shadows," Susan said, taking a breath between each syllable.

"What?"

Susan first pointed to the ground, and then to the sky. "The sun is in the wrong quadrant."

"That's a physical impossibility," Wayne said, without turning his head to look where Susan pointed. "I think I have a logical explanation for your confusion. I'm sure we didn't come straight up the face of the mountain. We simply must have moved farther around to one side or the other than we realized."

"The sun is the wrong size and the wrong colour," Susan said. "There are no clouds in the sky, yet the sun is so dim you can look right at it."

Wayne let out a long sigh of resignation.

"Have it your way then. I'm too tired to argue. Just out of curiosity, though, to what cosmic occurrence do you attribute the solar shift?"

"I don't have an answer, and there's no need for you to be sarcastic," Susan said.

"Maybe not, but why should I change now? Let's look for a positive ray of sunshine from this foreign star of yours. Perhaps we're doomed—you and I—for having passed the point of no return, but all may not yet be lost. If we hurry, there could still be time to tell the Professor."

A surefooted, straight-backed Professor Gates stepped into view, effortlessly twirling his heavy walking stick as though it weighed no more than a drinking straw.

"Tell me what, Earthlings? Welcome home?"

"What are you talking about, Professor?" Susan asked.

Before answering, he removed his jacket and rolled up his shirtsleeves to reveal the mottled skin of his forearms.

"You've crossed the line into my world—my universe. Let's see if I can explain your situation in words you'll understand. The prodigal professor has returned after a long sabbatical, bringing with him two fine specimens of an alien race."

The entity known to his students as Professor Gates paused to let that revelation sink into their consciousness before adding, "Don't worry, I'm not a vivisectionist. Some of my colleagues are, but I'll protect you from them for as long as I can. If I have my way, it will be many revolutions of my galaxy's sluggish star before they get their turn to examine you."

THE END

ABOUT THE AUTHOR

John H. Dromey was born in northeast Missouri. He enjoys reading—mysteries in particular—and writing in a variety of genres. He's had short fiction published in *Alfred Hitchcock's Mystery Magazine, Crimson Streets, Disturbed Digest, Stupefying Stories Showcase, Unfit Magazine*, and elsewhere, as well as in a number of anthologies including *Chilling Horror Short Stories* (Flame Tree Publishing, 2015).

SURVIVOR OF THE SPREADING MALIGNANCY by Emile Dayne

I

GOODKIND: "This is Officer Monroe, and I'm Officer Goodkind. Shall we start, Mr. Duvall?"

DUVALL: "You don't have to say my surname so theatrically, it really is my surname."

GOODKIND: "Ahem. Very well. It says in this report you claim to be from another planet."

DUVALL: "I claim no such thing. I only say that I have appeared here from another version of the Earth."

MONROE: "Another...dimension...you call it, apparently."

DUVALL: "Yes, for lack of better word."

MONROE: "And a rather strange word, you must admit."

DUVALL: "On reflection, perhaps it is. On my Earth it is the accepted term for such parallel worlds."

GOODKIND: "So on... your Earth... as you call it, you people may travel between the worlds?"

DUVALL: "Not at all. As far as I know this has only ever happened once. To me. However, the concept itself has existed in popular fiction for many years."

MONROE: "It sounds quite improbable, all of this."

DUVALL: "And yet here I am, talking to two officers instead of being locked up in a mental hospital, because the doctor in charge of my case was courageous enough to trust her intuition and do what I asked her to do."

MONROE: "Which is what?"

DUVALL: "Which is—as you know very well—to call a dentist who would testify that my teeth appear to have been fixed up with technology superior to the current level of dentistry in this society. This was, of course, a leap of faith on my part, I understand nothing of medicine, but it paid off."

GOODKIND: "This is, ahem, your only... proof."

DUVALL: "Only that and the clothes I arrived with, yes, which also should at some point be analysed. Maybe some differences in design or manufacture will be noticed, I don't know. Unfortunately, all electronics I had on me did not survive the transition between worlds."

MONROE: "The hospital informed us that what you now say were the remains of advanced technology, was in fact just broken down half-melted garbage, and that they simply threw it out."

GOODKIND: "We have been unable to locate it since."

DUVALL: "That's hardly my fault, is it?"

MONROE: "Can you perhaps tell our engineers how to make such technology?"

DUVALL: "I can't even tell you how telephones work. I'm not this kind of scientist."

GOODKIND: "You say you are an... anthropologist."

DUVALL: "Yes, the study of humankind, mainly pre-modern societies. Look, can I have a coffee and some water? Maybe cookies or something. I feel my sugar levels dropping."

GOODKIND: "Sugar levels dropping? What's this nonsense? Are you diabetic?"

MONROE: "Private! Bring the man some coffee and water and something to snack on."

GOODKIND: "Ahem. And so, Mr. Duvall, you were allegedly tasked with discovering the origin of some sort of mental affliction of the population on your...perpendicular Earth?"

DUVALL: "Yes. But it was not only psychological symptoms. I was part of a much larger team, or rather three teams, including physicists and engineers. We were all following lines of magnetic force and underground vibrations, which all appeared to converge on one place. And we converged there too."

MONROE: "In Asia."

DUVALL: "Yes."

II

MONROE: "Ah, the coffee and biscuits are here."

DUVALL: "Thank you."

MONROE: "Would you like a cigarette as well?"

DUVALL: "I quit seven years ago, and yes, I would very much like at least half a pack, thank you. But after the cookies."

GOODKIND: "It says in your file that you were first allegedly contacted by the government back in your alleged world, because of...certain pictures that people started drawing."

DUVALL: "Yes. Twelve years ago, I wrote a dissertation on the similarities of certain drawings and sculptures which seem to appear in very different civilizations just before they collapse."

GOODKIND: "What, like the Romans?"

DUVALL: "Well, not them. But certain Mesopotamian and Mesoamerican and Indus River cultures—yes."

GOODKIND: "Now, obviously you had Romans in your alleged perpendicular Earth. This means the same past. Why do you say our technological levels are different? Are you from a future version of our world?"

DUVALL: "I'm ready for that cigarette now. Ah, yes, thank you. Mm. So, no, not the future. In fact, going by calendars, you appear to be eight years ahead, compared to my home."

GOODKIND: "Then why is our technological level allegedly lower than yours?"

DUVALL: "How should I know? Someone didn't get born here, died too early there, someone else developed different interests. This changed history a little bit in a bunch of places, the differences accumulated. For example, I now know you people never had a Vietnam War after the Korean War. In my place the Vietnam War took over a decade and it really changed society. All of Western Society."

GOODKIND: "Oh yes, and changed how? I suppose we're all Bolsheviks now where you're from?"

DUVALL: "No, in fact the Soviet Union doesn't exist anymore back there, yet you still have it here."

MONROE: "I'm sure at a more appropriate time Mr. Duvall can provide us with a detailed description of the alleged differences between our worlds. Let's get back to the story. So you say you appeared here by accident?"

DUVALL: "Yes."

MONROE: "An accident which can't be replicated?"

DUVALL: "In the name of all that's holy let's hope so."

III

DUVALL: "I'll take another cigarette."

MONROE: "Help yourself."

GOODKIND: "Tell us how exactly you claim to have appeared here."

DUVALL: "As I said, my thesis was on what appeared to me to be an incredible overlap in the visual arts of ancient civilizations just before their disappearance. It wasn't received well. In fact, I didn't get my degree."

MONROE: "But you still believed in it."

DUVALL: "Yes I did. I rewrote my failed thesis into a commercial book and it became something of a success, in spite of the scientific community criticizing it mercilessly, when it bothered to notice it at all."

GOODKIND: "And yet you ended up

on a scientific research team."

DUVALL: "Yes."

GOODKIND: "How did that happen?"

DUVALL: "The government contacted me. They said they wanted to use my expertise."

GOODKIND: "Why?"

DUVALL: "Because children and mentally unstable adults all across the country, and indeed the world, had started drawing pictures and making crude sculptures which looked very much like the ones...like the photos of the ones I had placed in my book about the sudden end of ancient civilizations."

MONROE: "How fascinating. And what did you do?"

DUVALL: "I joined them, and the other scientists, as I said before, they detected certain lines of vibrations across the planet..."

GOODKIND: "Ahem. I believe you also mentioned magnetic waves."

DUVALL: "Lines. Lines of magnetism which overlapped more or less precisely with the...the lines of vibration."

GOODKIND: "All originating from a place in Asia."

DUVALL: "Yes. Sri Lanka. Probably still called Ceylon here."

MONROE: "You look like you need another cigarette."

DUVALL: "What I need is a dozen of stiff drinks, but I'll gladly have another cigarette, thanks."

MONROE: "It was that bad?"

DUVALL: "Very, very bad. The closer we got to the estimated epicentre, the... the crazier everything became."

IV

GOODKIND: "You mean the natives?"

DUVALL: "The local people yes, completely mad, brainwashed. Possessed. In fact, some of us started feeling not quite all right as well. Especially at night. But the locals had it much worse. Had to keep fighting them off."

MONROE: "Did you have soldiers with you?"

DUVALL: "Yes we did, later they added up to a whole squad, or I don't know what it's called, a platoon maybe, once the teams merged. And a good thing too. Everything was hostile. Not just the people. The animals, the insects, the vegetation, the weather. It was all... wrong. Alien."

MONROE: "Alien how?"

DUVALL: "Alien as shape, as colours, as...as behaviour."

GOODKIND: "But in the end you found the place where this was coming from."

DUVALL: "Yes, yes we did. It was an old hospital building. Cubical thing made from concrete. Overrun with terrible, moving vines, and pulsating moss, and clumps of disgusting mushrooms. And these small things, like rats, but much, much worse."

MONROE: "Go on."

DUVALL: "The very atmosphere around this place. So...thick. Warped. Inhuman. Repulsive. I refused...refused to approach it. My nerve finally broke. There and then my nerve broke. But the military guy. The second in command—Baxter got killed the day before, so the second in command, I don't remember his name—he forced me at gun point. Forced us all, I think. Nine of us left by that time. We entered."

V

DUVALL: "Inside it was hell. Foreign, throbbing things over the walls, the floor, the ceiling. Things...creatures... scurrying past. Most of them small, some of them bigger. Much bigger. Good thing machine guns worked there. Electronics didn't, but machine guns did. And grenades."

GOODKIND: "So did you, ahem, did you find what was causing it, ahem, causing all this?"

MONROE: "Yes, did you find it?"

DUVALL: "We found it. Four of us left by the time we found it. It was... I don't... I don't know how to describe it."

MONROE: "Was it people? A machine? Some creature?"

DUVALL: "Maybe it was a machine, maybe it was a creature. Maybe it was some huge alien fungus. I know there were people there too, but...absorbed. Just the outlines. The occasional face on a wall or a ceiling. All looking very much like...like the drawings."

GOODKIND: "The ones civilizations start to draw before they collapse, according to you?"

DUVALL: "According to my research, yes."

GOODKIND: "So, if people started drawing them, hence you being on that team, would you, ahem, would say your civilization was collapsing as well?"

DUVALL: "Not that I was aware. Some people would agree that it was collapsing, but then again someone's always saying that. Maybe it was still early days. Maybe the influence of that... malignant thing in that room...was still too weak."

MONROE: "Please continue your story. You reached the thing, or plant, or machine responsible."

DUVALL: "Imagine an enormous orchid made of flesh, or something very much like flesh, ringed by a fence of skeletal, constantly moving pistons, and in the middle of it all—a forest of tentacles, each as thick as a man and going right through the roof into upper floors."

MONROE: "I'd rather not imagine that, frankly."

DUVALL: "There was a light, a greenish light coming from under it. Not really light, more like a...a presence... and the colour was something different— all colours were different there—but if I were to describe it to a sane fellow human, I would call it a greenish light. I didn't know what it was back then, but now I think perhaps it signified a breach in the barrier separating different realities."

GOODKIND: "Ah, I believe we're getting closer to the way you say you appeared here?"

DUVALL: "Yes, yes we are. Long story short, soon there were just the two of us left, me and the squadron leader— without a squad anymore, of course— and he appeared to activate what I suspect was some portable nuclear device, or something similar. By this time I was completely numb—no panic, no fear—in fact almost welcoming...er..."

MONROE: "Almost welcoming death?"

DUVALL: "Oh no, almost welcoming being absorbed by that thing in the middle of the room. Its pull on my mind was tremendous by this point. I don't know how that soldier managed to fight it enough to go through the plan to blow it up. Brave man. Brave and strong."

GOODKIND: "But blow it up he did."

DUVALL: "Yes. Just as I had surrendered to the tentacles, and they were pulling me in, and I was right above a breach in the floor which shone with the...with the otherworldly green light. Boom!"

MONROE: "And you woke up here."

DUVALL: "Yes. Admittedly very crazed. It took me days to regain my sanity. Once again, the fact that the doctor in the hospital took the trouble to check my claims is fantastic. Now this is a woman who really follows the oath to help and heal."

VI

MONROE: "Well, that's, that's quite a story you have there, Mr. Duvall."

DUVALL: "I know, I know..."

GOODKIND: "You understand if we're more than a tad sceptical.

MONROE: Hey, are you all right?"

DUVALL: "Just... just overexcited maybe. You know. The memories."

GOODKIND: "If you feel you are capable of it, would you mind drawing for us some of those...uh...symbols, that started all this in the first place."

MONROE: "Yes, that would be, that's a great idea. Let's forget the ending of the story for now. Here's a pen, here, you can use the other side of this sheet..."

DUVALL: "All right. Now the most

common motif is a variation of this face, stonework, and also some bronze and gold carvings, right, and then also these figures, no, wait, the arms are longer, yes...."

GOODKIND: "Dear God."

DUVALL: "What?"

GOODKIND: "My son. Billy's been drawing these things all weekend."

MONROE: "Now wait a damn moment, let me see that. Oh No. My daughter too. Oh no."

DUVALL: "Oh no."

THE END

```
ABOUT THE AUTHOR

Emile Dayne writes intersectional
 pulp fiction influenced by the
 likes of Robert Bloch, Gerard de
 Villiers, Rachel Aaron, and Tom
              Sharpe.

  His short fiction has been
  published in Bards and Sages,
 Pseudopod, Phase2Magazine, Dark
 Discoveries, Encounters Magazine,
  Black Treacle, and others.

 He produces long fiction under
        various pen names.
```

THE LORDS OF IMAGINATION by JR Young

The lurid blaze greeted me that night as it had countless nights before. The blue flames danced deceptively amongst the outline of the imposing pines, guarding the flame of the kindlers from one unwillingly to brave the unknown of the forest beyond. One unwillingly such as I. For every night, I stood at the edge of madness and despair, gazing into that fathomless darkness, ears stinging from the impenetrable silence, in hopes of

catching but a note of the curious and seemingly musical crackling of the flames. For what strange wood can produce such sounds? The burning boughs moaned and hummed as if attempting to reveal, through solemn soliloquies in a language long lost, the intention of their ritual. For I had mastered the first phase, and the perilous popping of the embers heralded the second part of the dream. One I had not yet dared to conquer. Initially, I welcomed the blue beacon, preferring its eerie luminosity to the blinding black; however, as my nights contained within this fevered dreamworld continued, the once singular source of my sanity began to glow with fiendish ferocity. The wisping streaks of fire seemed to beckon me further into the darkened wood, while the fleeting warning of the boughs stayed me in terror. It was in those hours of fear that the primitive pulsating about my neck and infernal pounding within my head always began. My mind became clouded with thoughts that were not quite my own, and my eyes swelled with tears from sorrows forgotten. Before I could attempt to decipher the influx of emotions coursing through my being, I awoke as I always did, at the foot of my typewriter, cusping a most familiar flask, lacking any evidence of the previous nights' whiskey-infused stupor.

For the better part of my adult years I, Algernon Walker, have been an author of strange and weird fiction, selling my first horror piece to a magazine of similar sort at the age of seventeen. After receiving my degree in classic literature from Miskatonic University, I maintained my minor successes in work and life via my short stories. Though I lacked the luxury-laden life of the greats, my stories offered an escape, and I enjoyed making them. I did not experience my first real success in literature or life until I met Alice Bowen.

Alice was a studious southern belle who had managed to, contrary to the nature of the times and her young age, create and operate one of the more successful regional publishing companies. Our common interest in macabre tales sprouted endless conversations on ghouls, spectres, and all denizens of the dark. Our mutual musings soon grew to affection and, nearly to the day of the completion of my first novel, we were married. The novel was a success and our early years together were spent in blissful pursuits of trivial adventures throughout the known and unknown sights of the world. As we travelled, I continued to write my shorts, saving the laborious efforts of novel building for the solitude of my study. Alice was understanding of my reclusive nature; whether it be for business or the reclamation of my sanity, she was none the wiser. Writing was my true passion and when I was not lost within the halls of my own making, I was distant and cantankerous. Alice was beautiful, and it is true that we had much in common, but it was her position and prestige amongst the writing community which allured me most of all.

Nearly a decade passed since the completion of our wedding vows before our daughter, Rose, was born. Due to complications during the birth, Alice was ordered to a regime of strict bed rest and it fell upon me to care for them both. Writing was not only my predilection, but it was my only concern, you understand? My only love. As I have said, I enjoyed my time with Alice and I certainly thought our partnership was one beneficial to us both, but I had not sus-

pected this burdensome turn of events. The child was a raucous infant who wailed all hours of the night, wailed as if the sneering shadows that inhabited the tenebrous dark encircling the crib foretold unsettling fortunes. Between catering to the constant needs of Rose and Alice, my times within the halls of my fantasy were scarce, and did little to ease my agitation. I became tense and began to utter curses under my breath at every request Alice presented, for she had been lying about for months and I was no longer certain that she required my rather frequent assistance. It was ere such an outburst that Alice told me that she would not be returning to her work, and that she had full confidence in the strength of my writings and their ability to support our new family. She wished to stay at home with Rose and educate the child in the proper manner. The warm, reassuring smile that crossed her face portrayed, most accurately, her admiration and honesty, and it caused my blood to boil.

Soon after she informed me of her departure from her post, Alice began to recover physically and took over as the primary care-giver for the child. I was once again able to retire to my study, flask at my side, typewriter before me, and the quiet calm of the night at my back. I sat at the oaken desk, staring blankly at my idle hands. How could Alice lay such a financial burden at my feet? If I was to be the only source of income, I must produce! Imagination is the magical furnace, and this was not how it was fuelled... she was selfish. In this night of uncertainty, the dream came to me and never has it ceased henceforth. The tightness begins in my throat as my air is restricted, and the pain is so intense that my eyes bulge before I collapse from the shock. Every night I dream the same dream and every day I type the same sentences, an endlessly torturous and monotonous cycle. I have not left the study in what I can only assume to be weeks, nor have I seen Alice or heard the cries of young Rose. My heart says she has left me here to wallow in the wastes of my ineptitude and failures. Abandoned by my wife and publisher! How am I to pen my magnum opus if I do not devote my entire soul to the great work? It was only my intention to write the perfect story, and distractions were costly. She knew of my reclusive nature and, at one point paid heed to it.

There exists but one option to break the cycle, and that is to brave the deep, dark of the woods and venture towards the blazing flames. That is what I have managed to convince myself of in the weeks following my isolation. For all my attempts to exit the study that once conjured only serenity and peace of mind resulted in my collapse, leading me back to those wicked woods. I typed the same words I had typed over a dozen times before and downed the last dram of the whiskey from the flask. This was the cycle as I had come to know it. Soon the pain would follow. I clasped my hand over my throat and shut my eyes to keep them in my skull. The frigid wind of the forest swept over me and I opened my eyes to the dark. Long have I contemplated the source and cause of the fire in the woods, and my ponderings concluded that the blue flames were the sparks of my subconscious mind, the essence of my imagination waiting to be rediscovered and snatched from hollows of inactivity. This night I would brave the dark and seek my salvation.

I sat absorbed in the quiet of the place, awaiting the arrival of the musical cracklings. In time, the humming came as it always had, and I beheld the bursting flame. The fire, now emblazoned with renewed intensity, encouraged my first steps into the tree line. The limbs gnawed and scratched at my shoulders whilst the brambles and roots attempted to entangle my feet, yet onward still I marched. For how long I journeyed through the bush, I have no recollection. My body knew no exhaustion and with each stride I tried to imagine the new horrors I would introduce in my next novel, though none came to me. I could feel the irregular heat emanating from the pyre. It warmed my skin yet chilled my bones. The vines were lashing at me now, clawing as I was now closer than ever to achieving true greatness in my craft! The flames held the answer, and nothing would stop me now. I emerged from the last blockade of limbs into an odd, yet perfectly circled clearing. The firepit was there in front of me and the second phase of the dream was now complete. Though it was not the fire that my attention was fixed upon, but rather the awesome apparitions stoking its flames.

I recognized them all! Their words were etched into the marrow of my bones, stories sewn into the fabric of my soul! The masters of the macabre, and titans of horror tales. Poe, Howard, Bloch, Long, Hawthorne, Stoker and Lovecraft! I knew it was the fire that held the answer, for their works were the inspiration for my own stories. Now I would reclaim these fragments of my mind and be able to continue with my novel! I would be free of these damnable woods at last! I would be able to provide for Alice and Rose and break this writer's curse. The ghosts of the literary giants stood silent, surrounding the flame. Their gaze never left the pit. I paced around them, admiring everyone at first glance with boyish elation that soon decayed to apprehension. I did not believe in spirits and some of these men were not, to my knowledge, yet deceased. This pointed to dealings of the mind and such dealings should always be approached with caution.

The foreboding fear that festered in my gut had but seconds to manifest before my anxieties were to be demonstrated. The cult of creators turned their eyes from the blue flames and upon me for the first time. They began to part their ranks and beckoned me to enter their sacred circle. I stood by the side of the spectral Stoker, as all stares reverted to the fire. I followed their silent instruction. The flames painted the ground with a shade of blue that seemed to make the phantoms glow in the night. The ashes of the strange boughs burning within the pit were gelatinous, unsettling, and appeared to be crawling forth from their stone prison. The inferno roared, causing a shift in the tone of the musical sizzling, while blue sparks dotted the dark. The ashes cackled in a sinister symphony and conjoined with the baleful laughs now echoing from the monstrous mouths of my masters, causing the wonted tug about my neck to manifest.

I attempted to fall to my knees, which had become my customary ritual when plagued by the awful grip, but something held me firm. It was then I felt strands tighten around my neck and the pressure within my skull began to rise. My eyes remained transfixed upon the blazing inferno before me, and in those seconds before my neck snapped,

the flames returned my memories. I saw myself within my study, hanging from a noose, feet kicking involuntarily in defiance as life escaped me. I saw the remains of Rose and Alice strewn about the room and I recalled the sound of their screams as I butchered them. The gravity of my deeds was lost to me as I felt myself begin to slip into the dark yet again; alas, the noose did unknot, and I found myself back in the forest, back within the gaze of the overlords of my oppression.

The third phase of the dream was complete, as was my pilgrimage. The embers of the dying pyre flickered menacingly beneath the pale moonlight as my fate was made known to me. This was not the first time I had completed the dream. Not even close. I, Algernon Walker, have been made an eternal prisoner, constrained within a Hell of my own mental and spiritual construction. A remnant of an event long passed, a memory trapped within a nightmare, doomed to forever be mocked by the lords of my imagination...

I awoke as I always did, at the foot of my typewriter, cusping a most familiar flask, lacking any evidence of the previous night's whiskey-infused stupor.

THE END

```
          ABOUT THE AUTHOR
  J.R. Young is an author residing in
  South Carolina. His inspirations are
    Lovecraft, Poe, Howard, and the
    horror films of the late eighties
     and early nineties. He can be
         reached via email at
  jryoungfiction@gmail.com and twitter
            @JRYoungFiction.
```

THE FORGOTTEN SUPREMO by Mike Adamson

Making pizza was all Ricardo had ever been good at, but as skills went it was not one a young man would brag about. Sure, his friends told him he made the best pizza they ever tasted, but he knew they were just being nice. His college loan had been turned down, he saw no real outlet for his talents, and the future looked grim—an endless, going-nowhere grind as he made pizza after pizza, forever, in the dark little never-closing shop of Papa Giuseppe.

He was glad to have the job, especially in times so hard, and his family did not criticize him, but the darkly-handsome youth yearned for more—something beyond the dank, ancient brickwork of the Lower East Side. He swore some of these courts, streets and yards had not been torn down in hundreds of years; when the fog came in from the East River and street lights burned with sickly radiance, he could believe himself trapped in a timeless place where the past was a cloying millstone upon the present. The lights of Manhattan were a jeer to his aspirations, taunting him with all life might never hold, for how does a poor kid make good?

Old Papa Giuseppe had run his shop since 1950 in the very same premises, in a yard off the streets, a strange relic of the 18th century, where stone, timber and brick contorted in antiquated forms of roof, gable and window, such that when Ricardo went to work he felt he had stepped backward in time. The old man was stern, a patriarch of the old school, whose staff called him *sir* at all times, and Ricardo chafed under his clock-watching management. Time and motion, he would tell them, time and motion, so many minutes for this size pizza, so many for that.

Little wonder Ricardo feared he had begun to go, slowly but no less surely, quite mad.

The smell of cheese haunted his dreams, the stringy, elastic nature of the mozzarella lengthened eternally in the vault between waking and true rest, where he sliced pepperoni and opened canned pineapple seemingly forever. The radio was his only link to outside life, playing quietly on the shelf behind his work surface, in the dark nook beside the great wood-fired oven, whose chimney led up through the ancient brickwork, delivering its aromatic smoke to the New York sky. He would close his eyes and breathe deeply, trying not to smell the pizza around him, letting the music remind him another world existed at all. And sometimes he would open them again to find with a sickening start, he was in bed at home, merely reliving the monotony of work in the very time he should be free of it.

One evening in an uncommonly raw fall, Ricardo left the fifth-storey apartment he shared with four of his relatives, and made his way through the streets, coat fastened up and scarf around his face. Fog had come in from the river the last two nights and he felt so depressed he could hardly face work. A tug horn sounded out over the oily-still waters, mournful as a beast from ages past; he glanced up from the paving stones as the occasional passer-by hurried through the clammy evening, the fog flowing around iron railings and the brick of past centuries like the slithering tentacles of bizarre life. He turned at the alley into the yard, between once-grand buildings, hurried through lamplight past bins and trash, and found himself in the quaint world of the courtyard where time seemed suspended.

A few customers waited, the shop was bright and music played, and he rushed into the back as the old man's stern eye fell upon him. Two orders had just come through from the counter and he had time only to throw off coat, scarf and woollen hat before he was head-down at the bench, fingers flying in the studied patterns of the pizza chef.

But tonight was different.

I make so many, he'll never notice if I make one to take home.

The thought was heretical, it welcomed discovery and punishment, but it was radical, and the very rebelliousness of it appealed to Ricardo's tired soul.

I'll make one for the family... The best damn pizza they ever saw! Everything on—everything! It'll be a surprise...

An hour into his shift, thoughts of the finest bootleg supper making him smile, he was sent to assemble boxes. The old man's nephew usually did it but tonight they were short, and he was told to make up thirty boxes, quickly. They kept the packaging store in a room in the far back, it belonged to an adjoining building and was reached by a door-sized hole smashed through the wall. It was accessed from the alley by a door kept locked at all times other than when the delivery van wheezed into the confined space to offload five hundred more flat sheets of printed, double-corrugated card. The card was stacked neatly on a pallet, while finished, folded boxes rose in pillars on shelves against

the grubby, ancient bricks.

And here, it struck him. Perfect— he could hide his masterpiece in the raw box stacks, then collect it when he grabbed his coat at the end of shift. He was not sure yet how he would get it past the manager, but he would think of something. Maybe Suze, the girl on the register, would let him out the back way, she had charge of the keys on the night shift after old Papa had gone home. Yes, that would work...

As he made pizza through the evening, Ricardo felt almost giddy, his act of rebellion was unlike him and he sensed a slippery slope ahead. But more, there was also compulsion, for reasons he did not understand, he needed to do this, something deep and important urged him, and merely complying was the path of least resistance. Yes, he must do this. Make the grandest pizza of them all, and put it...there.

Papa was a staunch Catholic, but he knew the Old Ways. He had a *stregaria* grandmother, he knew more dwelled in the world than met human senses. Thus when he felt the slimy old walls of the yard closing in about him, when he stepped out to look up at the silver haze that blocked out the stars and shimmered sickly in the one street light between the buildings, he shuddered, crossed himself, and drove his hands deep in his pockets. This was an ill night, and no good would come of it. He backed into the shop and fumbled for his coat on the rack behind the counter.

"I'm going," he grunted, smoothing his great silver moustache with his gnarled knuckles. "Too cold for my old bones. You kids stay warm, y'here?" He seemed uncertain, almost afraid, made his way out in haste, barely lifting his hat to a lady customer as he went, an unknown failing on his part. Suze glanced at Ricardo with eyebrows up, then they settled in for the shift to midnight when Papa's second son came on as manager and they were replaced on till and chef's bench.

Trade slackened a bit and Ricardo planned his masterpiece. Not just a supreme, it would qualify as a garbage-pizza, everything on he could possibly cram aboard. It had to be family-size, that was a must. He set aside the makings, skimped a tad here and there on other orders, until he had materials in hand, and late, about eleven, he began.

With loving care he scattered the ham and cheese on the premade base, hands flew through the ritual of adding ingredients, and he barely heard the radio, humming instead a tune he could not name, a ponderous melody which evoked strange, dreamlike thoughts of a grandness far removed from old New York. It consumed him little by little, a feeling of warmth and something special, as if he performed a sacred duty and basked in the accompanying satisfaction. Now he no longer smelled the cheese, the ham, the condiments—instead, scents of garden perfume rose to his nostrils as if he walked an arbour in some distant land, under very different stars, among very different people.

As his hands continued the familiar motions of their own volition, his glazed eyes beheld long processions of robed men and women who moved with solemn step along quiet streets, up through terraced gardens toward a grand and monstrous temple, chanting softly the song he hummed, though he followed not the words. His mind floated with them up stairs of alabaster to doors of ungreened bronze, beyond which lay a holy of holies. Sacred fires crackled in great kraters, and the roar of gong and trumpet boomed in the night, worship echoing to the stars above—stars such as he had never imagined, and which struck deep into his marrow with an overwhelming sense of antiquity.

Here in Astropolis, the city at the heart of the universe, dwelled the ultimate force of all creation, that which was both entity and god, drinking in the adoration of countless multitudes, here and across the stars. Vast it was, and terrible, a beauty upon which none dared look, a horror to their senses should they imagine what lay behind the bottomless compulsion of their behaviour. Marinarius, they named it, that which swam in the endless maelstrom of space and time, the sea in which all things were born, lived and died. It was in all places, had endured since matter first came forth from energy, and had watched with cold, impersonal stare as life crawled from the oceans on a billion, billion worlds.

"Hail Marinarius," he found himself whispering as he carefully lifted his finished masterwork on the long paddle into the oven and set it to cook. Part of him would be at peace were it the last pizza he ever made, a prophetic notion at some level as he would be happy if it were the case.

He assembled the next order mechanically, seeing only the city beneath the stars, his head filled with the din and chaos of alien worship, and feeling behind it all the overwhelming urge to do this thing. No part of his rational mind questioned his insatiable need to make and hide the mother of all pizzas, he merely flowed through the motions and was satisfied.

At 11.38 it was done and he brought it from the oven at the same time as a double pepperoni. Two boxes lay side by side, one he filled and passed through to Suze in the front shop, the other he took with reverent care to the back premises, through the hole in the wall, and placed third from the bottom of the family size box stack. He was back in twenty seconds, his misdemeanour unnoticed, and a flush of deep fulfilment went through him. Abruptly, escaping with it seemed secondary, and a deep and formless conviction went through him that his life's purpose was spent. Such was nonsense, but in a lull between orders as he leaned against his bench, Suze came through and lay a hand on his shoulder.

"You okay?" she asked, concern in her hazel eyes under her blond hair. "Long night, huh?"

He nodded with a smile, but the cold emptiness swirling around his soul must have communicated to her, as she blanched and drew back her hand. "What's wrong?"

"I...don't know," he murmured. "I just get the feeling there's...no more. Nothing left to do."

"There could be an order before shift change."

He smiled, a thin, icy expression. "I don't mean work, Suze. Not sure what I mean."

"You need some sleep," she said sagely. "Papa works us too hard."

"Glad to have a job," he whispered, yet his eyes were distant, as if some wind from the distant stars howled about his soul.

And five minutes later they were in the courtyard between the tall, old buildings, Suze with her mobile at her ear, calling nine-one-one. Where the blaze had begun was a mystery, but a wall of flame had shot up to the ceiling, driving them out by its savage heat. Thinking forlornly of his masterpiece, Ricardo went back in and snatched the extinguisher from its nook, fought desperately but hopelessly until he heard collapsing stone and timber, and backed out, half-blinded by smoke. The nearest engine company was there in five minutes and brought savage jets of water to bare on the conflagration which was spreading to the second storey. Ricardo coughed raucously as he was treated by paramedics on the kerbside, out in the street beyond the alley.

All he could think was *it's gone... My masterpiece is gone.* And he grieved, with the soul of an artist for that which was beyond reclamation.

Yet gone it was not.

The shop was gutted, the next floor damaged, and the question of demolition hung heavy on the hearts of those responsible for the heritage-listed structures of the old East Side. The blaze was contained but whether the building was worth salvaging now was a matter for insurance investigators. Papa was there in the dawn light, rugged in his topcoat and pluming breath in the chill air, and the kids had been treated for smoke inhalation and shock. There the matter seemed to end, their jobs as gone as the shop. Yet the pizza remained.

The chamber in the adjoining

building had been blocked by falling brickwork before the fire could reach it and among the crisped but not yet burnt boxes, the super-supremo lay yet—abandoned, forgotten, beyond human ken, but not beyond the urgent attention of a very unhuman sentience.

Plans matured swiftly now, as that which had puppet-mastered the strange compulsions driving Ricardo had the time and anonymity in which to act. First it assured itself the ancient room would go unnoticed for some long while, then, with a chill and unearthly smile deep in its foul heart, it settled—to exude its filamentous nature across the membrane between the worlds, secreting its form in the third dimension as an extrusion of its higher dimensionality. Layer by layer, it took shape, deep in the moist, congealing layers of the pizza. It had guided Ricardo's hand from one ingredient to another, just the right amount of this, not too much of that, plenty of the other, setting in motion the correct conditions for its own eventual gestation.

Here was perfection, the balance of nutrients and moisture demanded for cellular genesis, in the fire-warmed dark of the old chamber, unseen and undisturbed. In two days the pizza was rotting perfectly, the corruption of its constituents fuelling exactly the rapid growth of the extramundane organism. First came aggregates of cells forming loose and random colonies, a green smear upon the mozzarella, there a rugged banding of collagen fibres reorganized from the ham, next a blooming of pre-organic tissues, the scaffolds for cells to come. Organs of curious function began to take shape among the wilting mushrooms, the decomposing tomato, here the core of a

digestive tract, tipped with a wickedly fanged orifice, there bundles of tentacular members that twitched and crawled long before the composite mass was complete. Maw after maw was born among the detritus as the pizza was consumed, its mass converting in abhorrent totality to the strange organism.

In a week it had outgrown the last dregs of Ricardo's masterwork and those tentacles reached through the ash and debris for the strong reek of rotting cheese and ham, the sourness of smashed and dried tomato paste among the tumbled brick and lumber—seeking tips found massive commercial size jars of the various ingredients and tumbled them from their shelves, smashed them and brought onion, garlic and bell peppers to the pulsing, ever-hungry mouths of the fetid mass that slobbered and crawled in the filth and stench. Next it found the handle of the cold room door, tentacles worried at it for long minutes until in a frenzy of frustration it found the angle and wrenched the chamber open. The power had been off a week, within was a perfect stew of decomposition—mouldy dough, greened ham in massive packages, cheese by the hundreds of pounds, four-gallon cans of tomato paste. All were tumbled, ripped open, and the abomination dragged itself into the store to gorge, stuffing itself moment by moment—growing, ever growing.

By day it heard the voices of humans in the courtyard, and watched psychically with the equivalent of narrowed eyes, a stare of hate that kept any from entering the shop as yet. Once it withdrew into the rear area as inspectors parted a tape barrier and shone lights around, searching for old electrical wiring, a gas connection, anything to explain the flare up. But they soon withdrew, their souls inexplicably chilled, and the thing returned to its gorging.

It knew not how long had gone by in the vast turning of the galaxies and the universe since the rise of the Younger Gods and their war upon it. Perhaps ten billion revolutions of this planet, but existence, reality, life and death had different meanings for those who were eternal, or for whom the geometries of Euclid held novel and arcane significances. Time was irrelevant, all that mattered was that the bridge between the spaces had been traversed, and now was the moment for the return of the Supremo Marinarius.

The rotting foodstuffs drew rats and the entity enjoyed its first hot blood, the thrill of sacrifice charging its veins in which flowed unholy ichors. How it had missed this! So long ago, yet it was but yesterday to its extradimensional memories, that endless tides of blood and flesh had crossed its altars, and would do so again. More and more, it scoured for the last morsels of edible filth in the charred ruin, gnawing the organic timber and consuming the cardboard boxes—anything it could digest, for it must grow! And the rats of New York make nightly march to the East Side from whence they returneth not, mesmerized by the unheard sirenical ululations of the entity from the stars.

Fall was giving way to early winter when it outgrew its confines and in the first white snow it burst forth, a titanic green abomination of rope-like tentacles and gnashing maws, flailing and rolling in its new world, snatching to it all it could reach, a dozen red eyes blazing like windows to hell. Here was fulfilment, as its siren song called the beings to their willing sacrifice, and they came by the scores and the hundreds, leaving their work to trudge through the snow into the alley and deliver themselves unto its waiting jaws. A crunching of bone and rending of living fibre filled the old courtyard, blood sprayed the brickwork as if the time of the berserkers had returned, and the hot, vital flesh fuelled its growth as never before. Soon the power of its mind washed outward from the city to the next and the next, and the little doings of humankind became as the dust of the balances. All heard and all made dreadful pilgrimage, free will surrendered to the implacable will of the one beyond time.

And, as its magnitude reached perfection and its hunger waned, Marinarius saw that it was good, and deemed the Earth a fit crucible for the resurrection of all that had been. Now would be reborn empire and dominion, and to its flailing tentacles would come all manner of beings from across the stars, to bend the knee and offer up adoration, in an ecstasy of revelation, for here was the being for whom the universe was made. Its temple would rise once more, arcane and superb, shrouding mysteries unfathomable to lesser lifeforms, as would rise the Orders—the Carbonarians, the Vegelarians, the Supremos and Pepperinians.

Earth would become the crossroads of the universe, shepherded by the Old God, and it would rejoice as the chosen world, rebirthplace and restoration of the imperishable Crustian faith.

THE END

ABOUT THE AUTHOR

Mike Adamson holds a PhD in archaeology from Flinders University of South Australia. After early aspirations in art and writing, Mike returned to study and secured degrees in both marine biology and archaeology. Mike currently lectures in anthropology, is a passionate photographer, a master-level hobbyist and journalist for international magazines.

THE CHRONOSPHERE by EW Farnsworth

I had only enough time to crawl into the Chronosphere, the time machine that had transported me to this god-forsaken future time. The fight in which I might have died but only received this slash on my left eyebrow was the crux to which I must return before my sight failed totally, as fail it must in any case. I needed only return to the time one hour before the alien creature entered my abode and slew my dear Maria then turned its attention on me.

For my besting it, the distributed, slithering creatures wreaked revenge on the whole human race. The alien presence and powers threatened to be invincible. I was convinced that if I returned, I could anticipate the creature's moves and destroy it utterly, so it could not communicate with its brethren—while keeping Maria alive. My eyesight was failing fast too. I knew from my calculations that I had just enough time to accomplish my objectives.

As a precaution against the unknown, I quickly jotted down my plan and entered the time machine. On its console, I dialled in the date of my transition, Independence Day, 2018. Pressing the button, I felt the tremor of the machine. I must have passed out, but I came to when Maria was brushing my hair away from my eyes.

"Maria," I told her, "We have no time to lose." I told her what she must do and gave her the instructions I had written. She had a thousand questions, but we had no time for a disquisition. I set the Chronosphere for the year 32,000. I had no idea whether the machine had the ability to carry someone that many years into the future, but I simply had to take the chance. Did I say that I have extraordinary size and strength—that of an Olympian weight lifter? I hoped that superhuman strength was sufficient to the task, but I would only be certain in the event.

At precisely the time the alien came slithering through my door, I seized it by its tentacles and flung it into the pre-set time machine. I slammed shut the door, fastening the device from the outside and activating the switch by the wireless control. The alien creature was conveyed instantly on its temporal journey into the distant future. As I saw the year-gauge rise to meet its objective, my eyesight failed entirely. I was totally blind. Maria wept as I groped the space to find her. My eyes were wide open, but I could not see—I knew for certain I would never see again.

All the time, Maria touched my face with her delicate hands, saying, "Your eyes, your beautiful green eyes. They cannot see now. Therefore, I will be your eyes. You shall be like the Greek ancient named Tiresias, the wisest human who ever lived, but blind."

I advised her to read out loud the

instructions I had written, so I could clarify any ambiguities. We had an urgent mission to eliminate the alien creature's race. I had already found the strength to foil its plan to eliminate humanity. "Surely," I thought, "I could defeat the others by the same stratagem. It will require developing other time machines and anticipating the aliens' synchronized movements, but I have nothing else on my agenda—and I have Maria to help me."

If I could manufacture the means to transport our common enemies to the distant reaches of time, we and our human race would be safe on this planet. Maria and I worked frantically—we were a two-person manufacturing team, and the parts for assembly were all around us. As I was blind, I used my hands to check the physical integrity of our chronospheres as they were completed in the barn I had converted for our purposes decades ago. Formerly I had been the laughing stock of the scientific community, today I would have been considered a hero. We built as if there was no tomorrow.

As we finally ran out of our stock of parts for our machines, I came up with an innovation that would magnify my machines' effects tenfold or more. I asked Maria to help me create a maze within which we would trap the tentacle beasts that came for us. She understood at once that we were going to create a replica of the Minoan labyrinth. However, instead of a Minotaur, our destroying devils were clones of my original chronosphere, calibrated to close after an alien's entry into it and forward the creature to a pre-set future time, each different from the rest. I planned to risk reusing the machines repeatedly.

The aliens did not take long to follow the path of the original of their species—the deadly specimen I had already sent far into the future. The maze was ready for them, and their collective intelligence was activated by the challenge I had provided. One by one, the slimy figures oozed into machines, which flawlessly closed on them and self-triggered their time-forwarding algorithm. I felt I was playing an old-fashioned video game as I checked the chronospheres that had been used and reset them for the next deployment. Maria kept careful records of the times we had programmed for the horrid beings' rebirths. My feverish imagination foresaw them emptied into unsustainable futures where they could do no humans harm.

Maria's records included visualizations of each alien, but all I could understand of them was her vivid descriptions of those images. She was good at conveying to me the attributes of the tentacle tribe in all their variations. For all their demonstrated intelligence, they seemed to have no way to comprehend the trap I had designed for them. They must have sensed somehow that their numbers were rapidly declining. Their motions slowed significantly while they deliberated what was happening and what to do.

I blame myself for not anticipating the aliens' studious avoidance of our labyrinth. They continued to ravage Earth but circumspectly only skirted the barn with our machines inside. Maria and I took stock. On the one hand, we were now safe from predation. On the other hand, we had less likelihood of expelling the aliens with our usual snare. Maria despaired of our surviving a long siege.

"Daniel," she pled, "We must do something to lure the aliens to their destruction. If they surround our position without invading it, all they need to do is wait and observe us die of starvation—or thirst."

I thought that through before I replied. "Maria, you are forgetting the power of our chronospheres. You have kept careful records of the times to which we have sent the enemy. We can always escape to intervals wherein no aliens lie. That, in turn, gives me an idea. We can visit interstitial times and, if there are humans then, warn of the alien creatures' powers and how to defeat them with our machines."

Mary, though frightened, was game for my new plan, but as with all spur-of-the-moment solutions, I had not figured on unintended consequences. During the execution of our plans, we encountered two problems. First, I was blind from macular degeneration, and I did not know how blindness prejudices humans against you. How many humans know the story of Tiresias as Maria did? Second, my chronosphere was a miraculous device with no sanction among humans. Who would trust the operations of a machine they could apprehend but did not fully comprehend?

As Maria and I cast ourselves forward to future time after future time, we faced the distrust and outright hostility of the humans we had pledged ourselves to save. Like Oedipus and his daughter Antigone, we appeared to speak truth yet were seldom believed. In our wake, we left doubts, suspicions and hostility. Rarely did we achieve our aims of creating disciples. In those instances, we taught the secrets of designing and operating chronospheres. We left operational prototypes. We drew up plans for sharing the mission of spreading the word about saving humans from aliens with the machine.

I was convinced we were making headway, but I had not counted on the learning capacity of the evil aliens we were trying to expose and defeat. Those tentacle creatures seemed to be attracted by humans who knew their hidden natures. As they increasingly had the habit of showing up where we were teaching and creating development labs, I deduced they were now using something like our chronospheres as we were. The only difference between them and us was our beneficent purpose of prolonging the duration of humans. Contrariwise, they were now using our technology against us. I decided to return with Maria to our labyrinth on Earth to undo the aliens' mastery of our technology.

"Daniel, do you think it's wise to return where we are known to be the greatest enemies of the invaders?"

"Maria, I know no other way to safeguard our program than to strike at the heart of the aliens' nest—and our labyrinth seems to be the most logical locus for attacking that aggregation. In fact, it's likely they have settled around our maze and gathered forces to besiege it."

When we returned, I discovered that my surmise was truth. The encirclement was complete, and the aliens were preparing to make their assault. As a result, we found ourselves surrounded, but not yet under pressure from alien attack. I knew we could not hope to defeat the enormous army that was massing to rush our position. My thought was to find a way to leave a fatal surprise for the aliens before they realized it meant their annihilation.

I made a snap decision and told Maria we were going back in time to Los Alamos where the first atom bomb was tested. I had read that five bombs, not one, were ready for detonation on that historical occasion. One was for the test. Two were for use against Japan. The other two were not obligated. I explained my plan to Maria, so she could support my plea to Dr. Oppenheimer.

We arrived at Los Alamos one day prior to the test. Maria led me to the technical project leader. She made our case for appropriation of one bomb.

"I understand your need, but you are asking to take one of our precious weapons without really knowing what it can do."

I explained to Oppenheimer what the test would reveal and what would happen afterward. My plea struck his heart, and he gave us permission to take one bomb into our chronosphere. It barely fitted in our machine, and Oppenheimer's team set it to detonate in two hours. I sent the chronosphere with the bomb back to the maze just as the aliens began their attack. Maria and I did not see the result of the atomic explosion, but we guessed at its effects: a mushroom cloud, all bright and powerful. From the edges of the expanding form, tentacles spilled as from a fountain. The maze was destroyed along with the alien menace.

Dr. Oppenheimer found a place for us at the test range of Los Alamos. I did not see the historic blast, but I felt its heat and light from a distance. Maria told me what she had seen, and the vision changed her life. When we left Los Alamos, we were under strict restraint against divulging what we had seen.

We were allowed to tell the story of the coming of the aliens at some future time. Maria led me through the cities where Americans were protesting the use of the atomic bombs at Hiroshima and Nagasaki. We told our incredible story of the utility of the same kind of weapons against a far greater threat from aliens in the future.

Just as we had been disbelieved as we battled to tell about the tentacled creatures, so now we were reviled as troublemakers who defended the worst weapons imaginable. I finally withdrew from my self-proclaimed mission with Maria to build another version of my chronosphere. What did I care whether we were believed? We had seen the future clearly and done the right thing as we understood it. We longed to return to our maze, but in a time long after the blast we had arranged—when the nuclear risks were minimal, and the blue cornflowers bloomed at the blast site.

Would we find evidence of the aliens at our maze? I certainly hoped not. Still, we were prepared instantly to reprogram our travel to some distant future if something had gone awry. Maria was happy if we remained together. I could not see her face, but she conveyed her happiness in her voice and her touch. Of course, her hands constructed the new chronosphere, and the novelties I incorporated in its design anticipated the evolution of both humans and aliens. One day, I thought to press outward to the limits of time itself. That would require a new manner of dial altogether.

I will design the new chronometer

and Maria will build to my specification. Though I cannot see, I know how the thing should work. It will work, as the last I built did, or better.

THE END

ABOUT THE AUTHOR

Dr. Wilson F. Engel, III, writing as E. W. Farnsworth, lives and writes in Arizona. E. W. Farnsworth has just signed a contract for the publication of his story, "The Seventh Figure," with Night Picnic Press LLC. The story will appear in English (with a Russian translation!) in Night Picnic Journal 2: 2 in early 2019. See www.ewfarnsworth.com

THE BLOODY RULE OF THE CATALAN COMPANY by Sergio Palumbo, edited by Michele Dutcher

They arrived around midday and immediately began doing what they normally did, plundering and causing death without reason or regret. Wearing little to no armour, growing their hair long, with dirty beards, most of those mercenaries used a spear and a short stabbing sword to do their dirty work, and all of them had wild looks on their faces as they moved quickly, beating and killing everyone they saw. After the first wave came their carts, horses and young serfs. And only a few hours after their first passage through the village, everything had been completely turned around, with smoke and the cries of the injured or the dying filling the air.

With swords in their hands, those plunderers thought—or simply hoped—that their attack would be so much of a surprise that they wouldn't find much opposition. How could the attacked fight back, after all, as this was a small village where only poor peasants and women lived? There was the constant sound of arrows sinking into the wood houses, whenever they didn't hit some villager's chest or face. Cries of suffering men and continuous bloodshed filled the place, seemingly inescapable.

"Follow me, men!" shouted a powerful voice. The massive figure wore outdated armour with full-length sleeves and a long and narrow helmet. He had a pointed chestnut beard, and he urged the younger men to move ahead rapidly, inciting those beside him to rush forward while ignoring the desperate cries for help that came from wounded villagers. "Straight to the houses, take all you can, and kill anyone you meet at once! Hernández, Gerard, without respite!"

He wasn't a captain but he did what he had been ordered to do by his leader. He seemed capable of bringing out and strengthening the most dangerous wishes that resided in the minds of the warriors who followed him. Given the high number of people he had already murdered or was about to kill, he certainly knew how to use his weapon. It was his enemies—who didn't seem to be enemies at all, being more like sheep that fell to the ground as the metal of their spears touched the sides of their necks—who directly witnessed his prowess against the weak. You could also see everywhere a mix of armoured and un-mailed men endlessly moving across the terrain, and in the end only the ones who had been unarmed remained lifeless when the battle was over.

You could also see the children who were sons and daughters of the desperate villagers—and had already become orphans—running everywhere, though they wouldn't be starving in the streets, most likely, as at the end of that assault all of them were going to be dead...

How could it be different, after all? The poor community living in the village of old Kotyli, located in northern Greece, was only made up of a few houses, some small sheds, and peasants or herders who tried to eke out a living by working hard in the fields. The climate had always been hard in these surroundings, changing from semi-humid with floods and then drought during winter and summer, respectively, due to the presence of depressions in the small valleys of the area. The locals had few resources and almost no money, of course, but the lack of material goods was appeased by the presence of what every village in the area was well endowed with: food and Greek women, both young and old, to be taken and sold as slaves. Or to be made use of for different, more immediate and lustful purposes that were on the minds of those hot-headed, cruel newcomers.

Almogavars like them came mainly from the mountainous regions of Aragon. As they were frontiersmen and foot-soldiers, most of them wore no armour, dressed in skins, were shod with *abarcas*, sort of brogues, and made use of spears or of swords. Their discipline and ferocity, the force with which they hurled their pointed tools of death had given them a very ruthless reputation. They usually fought against cavalry by attacking horses first instead of knights. Once the knight was on the ground he was an easy target for the Almogavars, which allowed them to satisfy their baser impulses. The origin

of the word Almogavar itself seemed to be—like all Iberian words beginning with the prefix 'al'—derived from the Arabic language, whose meaning was uncertain to the local populace. The captain of the large squadron—called Martín—was known in Catalan as 'Almogaten', also from an Arabic term which meant 'raider' or 'devastator'. True to the name... Part of the battle cry of the Almogavars themselves was: 'War and plunder, there are no greater pleasures! The wild beasts are hungry!' Those words had become well-known by the peasants, citizens and soldiers throughout the entire region.

However, their presence in the countryside had started under different circumstances and with the best of intentions by the Emperor of Byzantium who had hired the Catalan Company in September 1303. It was also called the Grand Company, and was a large group of cruel militiamen, to be of help against the Turks. Other accounts had it that, after having been raised to fight as mercenaries for the Kingdom of Sicily for decades, bringing much suffering and hard losses to all the local population, it was a pirate who later joined the Catalan Company and worked his way up to become its main leader in the end, bringing his men to these parts of Eastern Europe.

Over the course of the war against the Turks, their unruliness along with their continuous demands for more money and new lands became unbearable to the Emperor himself who decided, in the end, to get rid of those bloody warriors who might one day prove to be a threat to his rule. Anyway, it was the Grand Company itself that defeated the Byzantine army that was sent to wipe it out. Other smaller confrontations followed, but what was left of a largely decimated company, plus the addition of a significant number of disaffected Turkish deserters, became a group of warriors made up of only 206 horsemen and 1,256 foot soldiers with no clear leader. It began spreading its influence by separating into squadrons across a vast territory that remained in ruin for the next two years. This was how they had earned their predominance throughout the region of Thrace, and not only here. After that, the Almogavars had turned to brutal violence, making their presence intolerable to the poor population of those Byzantine lands. It is said that there was no village, urban area nor farm that wasn't subjected to their plundering or attack.

In reality, the locals agreed upon the fact that the Rhodopes, regardless of being the oldest mountain range of the country, had never seen such fierce and bloody raiders before, although their incredibly deep rivers and immense caverns, that held abundant water reserves and many springs and lakes, had witnessed in the ancient past the passage of many peoples coming from abroad wanting to conquer the area or to settle nearby.

The cries of agony continued throughout the small village as the heartless mercenaries entered every single house and exited soon after with plunder in their hands, leaving blood and silence at their back. When the men didn't find enough inside, they turned their mind to other ways of providing food and approached the few slim donkeys they happened to spot around the houses, bashing them in the head using hammers—making them die a slow, agonizing death. It was the cheapest method, many said, as their swords were ready to cut meat out of those remains.

One old man was beaten for half an hour, just because he seemed to have looked angrily at one of the militiamen. Then the offended foot-soldier himself approached the target of his hatred with a dirty knife in his dirty hands and sliced the old man's eye out of the wrinkled face of the screaming herder, leaving him on the ground in desperate pain with blood spurting down his face and onto the ground.

As usually happened when the squadron of their company got to a place like Kotyli—which was full only of poor peasants or old citizens that could not properly defend themselves—a show of power and evil actions started. Using unforgiving steel, intestines were unwound, ears cut off, brains opened and spurts of their remains were left on the stone walls of the one-storey houses that dotted the main street. Other horrible and certainly regrettable things also happened during those first hours after they came, but how many heads were severed and bodies were punctured or battered is a merciless process that doesn't deserve a full description.

This wasn't what Martín, the captain, was presently overseeing. In a way, apart from the five locals he had personally dealt with, it seemed that he did not have much time to watch the massacre of the village folk, as his interest was focused on the goods, supplies and food which could be plundered and taken to a single house—that had been previously emptied by throwing its owners on the street. This house became a kind of headquarters, where all of his men would share and distribute the boodle according to the rules. Of course, they all knew that keeping all that food for themselves was just another way to kill—although not by means of their blade—those poor villagers who might be left wounded, who would soon starve because of the lack of vegetables, meat and the likes when winter arrived.

The tall dark-haired captain, wearing blue clothing, with orange and claret colours under his armour, didn't even stop when he noticed the corpse of an infant among the dead at the side of the dusty path. Such things didn't matter to him, they had never mattered. His thoughts were clear about it all: leave alive a single angry villager that had been wronged or let him grow up and become capable of yielding a weapon one day, and he might come by, maybe with armed sons or other friends of his, to get his vengeance when you least expected an attack. It was something that his merciless instructors had always told him, and he always kept it in mind.

On the other hand, the man had never learned any respect for the weak, which was something completely alien to his way of behaving, living and thinking. This, too, the Catalan captain shared in common with the rest of the members of the squadron of his company, undoubtedly. Their main law was that the wrongdoers that were part of their group and worked for their own good had always to be protected, and everyone else could go to hell! There were no innocent people, it was just them and all the others. The others, of course, were just targets to be plundered or enemies to be met on the battlefield. However, in a very few cases, they could become allies for a common interest, too. But he didn't give those alliances

too much credence, as none of the few ones he had entered into had lasted for long. The truth was that, in most cases, it had been they themselves who had chosen to betray the others, always for profit, better income or for opportunities of the moment. The Grand Company was certainly notorious for making enemies of its friends.

The village of old Kotyli was made up only of a few meagre homes built on the northern slope. The villagers knew perfectly well that they could not rely on distant authorities to afford them protection, so their ancestors had hit on a solution which was meant to shield them from their possible enemies for hundreds of years, thus making the inhabited area into the image of a sort of fortress. Instead of wooden roofs these small buildings had become flat-roofed to prevent them from being assaulted by fiery arrows. Sheds and dwellings were built on terraces close to old ones so eventually the village encircled itself in stone, with the obvious hope that the architectural combination itself would prove a worthy defence system with the whole much stronger than its individual parts.

Sad to say, none of that had proved to be of any use today. And the number of the villagers was decreasing by the minute, certainly all of them would be dead soon if the captain himself didn't decide to leave just a few alive. Not out of compassion, but if it suited his own purposes.

While the onslaught was going on, the chestnut eyes of the stony Almogaten happened to spot what might be, and it undoubtedly looked like, the entrance of some caves, though with an unusual shape, situated at the far end of the village. This had put the thought into his mind that 'These are really some poor, stupid, worthless people—but even the most stupid individuals can display a bit of cunningness, at times, especially if they are old enough. What if all they own is not within these poor houses? What if they put their valuables, whatever those might be, and additional food supplies inside those caves?' This was enough to leave a few villagers alive, for now, so that they could tell him what might be hidden in the caves...before dying!

There was only one run-down house, even worse than the others at first sight, near the entrance of the caves themselves. The captain ordered the few villagers still alive to point out the owner of that house, if he happened to still be among them in this world. It was a child with blood on his legs who raised his trembling hands and pointed to a bald-headed old man who could barely stand. This one was worried when all of the wild eyes of the militiamen turned to him, and he certainly thought that his time to die had arrived, when the voice of Martin addressed him.

"Do you live in that place?"

"Yes, sir... I do live there... please..." the other replied in a sorry tone.

"Enough with entreaties or prayers, old man!" The Almogaten moved forward and his brutal slap struck the bony face that was caught unawares. "Just answer my question! I don't understand all the words in your pitiful language and I don't want to hear you say anything more than it is necessary."

"Yes, yes..."

"What kind of work you do there? Are you a herder?" a hurried

Martin continued.

"I sell meat... I feed sheep, then kill them... I sell their meat..." the man explained.

"And are you rich? Be certain not to be lying to me!"

"I... I'm not, actually... you can see how poorly dressed I am."

"I see how you dress..." the Almogaten said, condescending to glance at him. "So, tell me something about those caves up there... Are those your caves? And is that an entrance, not far from your home?"

"Yes, there are caves from that point on... down the mountains..."

"Are there people down there, too? Villagers who escaped before we arrived?" Martin eyed the other with an angry look.

"I...well, I don't...know..."

Another brutal slap was followed by some curses from the captain. "I told you to make sure you weren't lying to me!"

"Really... I don't know..." the other couldn't help say, repeating what he had told him before.

"Alright... Did you see anyone go in there when we arrived? Did you see any villagers go in that entrance?"

"No... I... didn't... but... actually..."

"But? What are you trying to say? Go on!" the Catalan pressed him.

"At times... I hear voices... coming from the caves... from deep underground..."

Voices? Maybe people who had escaped when they came here and preferred to stay in hiding until the newcomers were gone...These thoughts came to the captain as he kept looking at the fearful old man. Maybe they had also taken their valuables and food with them! "Voices, you said?"

"Yes, yes... voices, otherworldly words... please, please..." his words had become unbearable now. "I also hear some terrifying sounds, at times... I don't know what they are... what they mean..."

Perhaps there were really people living there, the Almogaten considered, his mouth turned into a broad grin. Maybe there were villagers who knew about raiders like them in the area, who had preferred to stay completely away from the open sight and live secluded for weeks, waiting for better times... It might be possible, why not?

They needed to be sure whether or not those caves were clear.

"Alright, form a group of five men to come with me," a hurried Martin told the muscled fair-haired Aleix, his Alférez, who stood nearby. "You'll be one of the group, and we'll bring with us this old man as well. Let's see if what he says is really true... there might be riches, or at least more food down there. Keep your swords ready... if there are people in those caves, they might also be armed."

"Aye, captain! You, Hernández, and you two, Gerard and Alcácer. Get ready and come with us. We'll go up that entrance to the caves, immediately!" the bearded and dirty Alférez ordered the mercenaries who were next to him.

So, after taking all of the weapons and equipment that might prove useful during their underground journey, the group of plunderers—accompanied by the old man—prepared to leave that

overcast sky for a much darker setting. The five mercenaries easily hiked up to the home of the aged villager who was following them. The ground floor seemed to have been used to store animals, storage and tools, while the left side appeared to have some notable carved decorations outside. The side and back walls were windowless. After getting past the house, the first two men who led the way each took one of the torches that had been previously prepared for their first trip into the underworld, reached the entrance to the cavern—that closely looked like a strange shape of both horse and bird of prey—and went in.

From the beginning, after the first few steps, the upper part of those caves, faintly lit up by their torches' weak fires, appeared a forbidding, unpleasant place. How could anyone live inside there for any length of time? the captain wondered, but then he thought that maybe, if there were really individuals hidden down there, they probably didn't stay inside all the time, just for whatever time was necessary, so as not to attract unwanted attention. Maybe they used the caverns to limit the hours they stayed in the open.

The cave chambers appeared to be very wide, possibly of volcanic origin, as the group started looking around. After a few thousand feet, they reached a crevice where some lower, darker areas below them were visible. This was the point that, probably, most people would have turned back. Anyway, if some villagers knew about this cave and its branches, this might also mean that they could have chosen to take their chances and stay safe in the mountainous deeps, distancing themselves from any barbaric raiders that came to plunder all of their houses outside.

The temperature inside that cavernous, immeasurable space was much more pleasant than outside, the Almogaten remarked, although there seemed to be something strange, difficult to explain, in there. Despite the lack of chill, they could sense an unusual discomfort that grew more and more as the group went down further and deeper. What might it be? Fear, or uncertainty about the unknown place they were going through? This was hard to say, as they all were hardened men at arms, and merciless raiders who had undergone many situations worse than this, having fought against fierce adversaries without retreating, even when the time came to slaughter young villagers in the streets or kill boys who weren't even 14-years-old on the battlefield. So, what was it that made them so afraid?

It was as if those dark caves whose obscure walls surrounded the group gave them all a despondent feeling. But the captain knew he needn't be afraid—at least not for now. However, he could see the same doubt, the same wavering, in the eyes of his men, which he had never seen before.

"I can see a flickering light in the distance, captain." It was Aleix who spoke all in a sudden. "This is really strange... maybe there really are people living down here, you were right!"

"I don't see any lights..." the old villager said, but he immediately regretted that he had dared speak, as no mercenary had addressed him.

"Be quiet, old man!" an angered Almogaten abruptly ordered. "I think you have good eyes as usual, Alférez...

There's something further on, this way, follow me..."

The villager looked ahead again, but he saw no light. What were they were talking about? Though, on this occasion, he preferred to remain silent and didn't object.

"I hear a voice, too..." one of the mercenaries, called Gerard, unexpectedly said.

'A voice?' the old man wondered, without letting a single word out of his mouth. He didn't hear anything... was it because he was old and his hearing was bad?

Martin squinted and tried his best to focus on any sounds that were coming from below. And, finally, he heard it!

A voice full of strange, alien words rose up from the deep darkness, reaching the ears of all the men at that moment. Or was that whisper only in their minds? Only the villager didn't seem to notice it at the moment.

"Coooome... Coooome to my sanctuary... in these forgotten lands..." The message came like a cold wind that passed through the blackness which surrounded them, piercing through the rocks and touching their souls. It didn't appear to be a human tone at all, and what was said seemed to be made up of unusual sounds, mixed up with rock bursts and venting of gases, that didn't resemble any known language, although they all understood its meaning.

"I have stayed here for many more centuries that yooooou could never imagine... There has not been enough challenge here to attract my attention for a very long time... only weak humans, poooor villagers that were never involved in dark deeds. Just the killing of sheep, at times, or the killing of chickens in order to eat them, but nothing more... Yoooou, instead, and yoooour bloody actions have reawakened me... yoooou have enticed my interest..."

The group of mercenaries weren't capable of properly reacting to those strange words. What was that thing talking to them? Was it a sorcerer who practiced who knows what forbidden arts, living by himself away from the world of his own kind in the caverns?

"Yoooou seem to be so skilled with arms and hands, yoooou look at people the same way predatory birds look at their helpless prey... yoooou also are eager to beat animals, tormenting them constantly uuuuntil they die... "

The singsong speech kept going, very badly reaching their ears, taking hold of their minds.

"So, yoooou were all united and entirely led under yoooour purpose to abuse and torture people living in the village near the place where I myself live, and yoooou'll be perfect pawns to be used by me for my purposes..."

The captain tried to raise a question, undoubtedly he wanted to know who, or what, the hidden proprietor of that voice was, but he simply couldn't form the words in his mouth. Though, the answer came to him even before he could move his lips.

"I am one of the Outer Gods. The ones like me live longer than yoooou could ever imagine... Outer Gods, like me, can stay silent, in the deeper recesses of this or other worlds, wherever we decide to travel. Superior beings, like me, seem to be without life for very long periods... our purposes and interests are not for yoooou to know... Yog-Sothoth is my name, though ancient men have called me Aletheia, The End of Darkness. And I am also the gate, the key and guardian of the gate. Past, present, future, all are one in me, the ancient Yog-Sothoth. Outer Gods, like me, are out of yoooour reach and far above yoooour comprehension for now and probably forever... yoooou are just humans, after all, and yoooour limits are clearly obvious..."

The terrified Almogaten was still speechless, and very worried. Gods, here, in the darkness of the underground? How? Why? "If this is true, I want to know everything...I want to see you!"

It was at that time that Yog-Sothoth, or Aletheia, or The End of Darkness, as he was known, manifested as vast spirals of several giant hands with a single ghastly eye in each palm. Those hands with those eyes approached the mercenaries, touched their skin, very painfully entering their body while causing unbearable suffering to their souls. Deep wounds were also made to them, injuries that were not visible on the outer stratified layers of flattened cells that covered the entire structure of a human being, though the damages that came from them were even crueller, and never meant to be quelled, nor suppressible. Whatsoever it might be possible...

"My tendrils are able to ensnare living beings like yoooou, replacing their spinal bone with my fluid... This has just happened to yoooou! From now on, yoooou'll be my unwilling servants who will be forced to do as I order, living a life that is no more yoooours and acting, attacking or killing among yoooourself as I please. It is time for a bloody Puppet Play that I'll enjoy watching as yoooou harm yourselves or cut each other's bodies according to my will, using yoooour pointed swords! Yoooou are now mine alone!"

As the mercenaries emerged from the dream of sorrow they had been thrust into some moments ago—though it was no dream at all, and the pain that was inside them was unending... They understood at once what the creature was telling them, as their arms and legs started to move to the right and to the left, though unwillingly, and with no way to stop or to prevent themselves from behaving according to the will of this old, truly merciless god.

"I sensed such cruelty in yoooou, when yoooou came near this place, up there on the surface... This cruelty is something that always attracts my interest, that awakens me... This is certainly better than those poooor sheep living in that village whose life has never given me a profound sensation, nor ever attracted my interest. In fact I never laid my many eyes on them so far, the same as the stones that are spread all around here mean nothing to me... At times I sensed some bloody actions, the killing of an animal to be used as meat... but it wasn't enough to awaken me. I feed on something deeper, crueller and bloodier than that! And yoooou are bloody, unredeemable, hopeless and cruel! Therefore, yoooou'll be a perfect subject for my pleasure... Have yoooou seen small wooden soldiers human children use to play war with? Well, prepare to be my toys for the next game that will be played according to my rules. And when it is over, be sure that no one will ever care about yoooou or try to find yoooou, just as a child doesn't care about poooor broken toys that lay lifeless on the ground after he stops playing..." Yog-Sothoth, or Aletheia, or The End of Darkness, growled.

The unbelieving and horrified mercenaries began to fight and the ferocious confrontation among themselves started. Blood was soon everywhere, streaking the walls all around, though it was not visible because of the darkness of the place that became even more terrifying after the torches were dropped to the ground and their light was put out. But the wild battle to the death didn't stop and the exchange of piercing lunges, blows and attacks continued in the blackness, through which only the cries of pain and the clamour of suffering of the pitilessly wounded seemed capable of occasionally emerging.

As the unarmed old villager hurried out as quickly as his tired legs might bring him out of those caves, that bloody confrontation endured. Then, the alien utterance spoke again, at the top of its voice, and his invitation was meant now for the remaining mercenaries that had stayed on the surface, outside of those cavernous deeps of despair.

"Coooome... Coooome on... yoooou others, too, coooome to my hideout... and bring yoooour weapons... we'll be having fun. Me, for sure, for a while, and yoooou, just before dying... Then I'll sleep again, a long slumber, until somebody else like yoooou, urged by cruelty, wickedness and lack of humanity coooomes to this cavernous place, and entertains me again..."

The cavernous space carved through dark rocks was now full of blood, bowels, severed heads and spurts of human tissues. It was a pity that only the long-forgotten Outer God could see those details in the blackness, that only such unearthly senses could enjoy it.

Though, much more will be following soon. Much to the delight of the creature from another reality, before coming back to a good slumber. Who knows for how long...?

Until the right day came to start again the long journey across time and space.

THE END

```
        ABOUT THE AUTHOR
Sergio 'ente per ente' Palumbo is an
Italian public servant who graduated
from Law School working in the pub-
lic real estate branch. He has pub-
lished a Fantasy RolePlaying illus-
trated Manual, WarBlades, of more
than 700 pages. He was also a co-Ed-
itor, together with Mrs. Michele
DUTCHER, of the Steampunk Anthology
"Steam-powered Dream Engines", pub-
lished in March 2018 by Rogue Planet
Press. His new anthology "Fantastic
Savannahs and Jungles" is now avail-
able from the same publisher.
```

FORGET ME NOT by Dean Wirth

1980

Ivan Korzack believed things left behind would eventually be forgotten, no matter how horrible. The squalor and bitterness of the Warsaw ghetto Ivan and his wife had experienced was arguably in their past. In desperation he had searched for dead rats, dogs and cats for sustenance to bring home. The worst was the warmer months when the decomposition and fetidness were in their full atrocious colourations. In the cold bitter winter there were at least no flies on the frozen carcases which he carried back in a burlap sack.

Now in the new world he approached the building of his employment every single day thinking how he hated this new life, too. The oppressive boss called Feldman humiliated him daily, commanding him to do things he never thought possible. It was not a choice; when his boss unzipped he had to do as he asked. Every lunch hour this happened, when this fat disgusting Feldman would come back from his meal.

He had walked out of a life of near starvation into a life of shame and misery. He lowered his gaze to the tiled floor as the familiar uneasiness set in. Having to support his expectant wife Kalena who neither spoke nor understood the languages English or French, chaining her to the home in Montreal and him to this actuality. They were devoid of any joy in the cramped apartment on la rue Bleury on the east side of downtown Montreal.

He could never tell Kalena of what happened at work every day. They lived in their small run-down apartment, a walk up that sat over a Chinese restaurant. The outside wooden stairs were very treacherous and slippery in winter, but at least it offered peace and quiet as the sole adjacent suite was unrented, also it was convenient to walk to work to as it was just a few blocks from the Belmont Building that sat squarely on la rue Aylmer.

He usually looked to his feet as he entered the building, trying to remain rooted in the real world. Walking to the Belmont was walking into a hall of shame. Something else was in this furrier building that was not right, it went beyond the impressions of dead pelts and hides with glass eyes peering out of the display cases. A foulness lurked.

The Belmont stood between De Maisonneuve and la Rue Mayor, directly to the north of Saint James United church. The post-world war two industrial block with its hundreds of vertical meshed windows towered over this gothic house of worship. Belmont Furs was once the whole of the building, there still was the prominent Belmont sign at main entrance so that the building, though dust and grit had tarnished its shine. In 1980 was it was still referred to as "The Belmont". Inside the white-streaked brown marble walls the lobby boasted inlaid glass display cases housing stuffed beaver, stoat and mink set on natural settings with painted backgrounds. Yellowed portraits of models wearing fur in sensual rapture hung on the walls. The white ermine, the brown stoat decorated the vast lobby. Embalmed and mounted, from stitched faces the display animals peered out their realistic glass-bead eyes frozen in poses glued to their pieces of timber. During business hours the lobby's manually-operated freight elevator to the East as well as the automated business elevator to the West selectively drew in and transported people.

A trophy shop was tucked in on the second floor among the white smocked workers pushing metal racks with coats and wooden carts loaded with damaged pelts and sample pieces. They used the clunky wooden gated freight and not the business elevator which was at the west side. The low levels of the building, B2 and B1, were used as extra storage for the businesses. The lockers down here were rarely padlocked as the furriers all knew each other and there was little or no value to these goods.

The janitor was constantly emptying the lobby ashtrays of cigar butts and wrappers of the visitors and people of the building. After the evening cleaners had buffed the patterned marble floor and gone home, the lobby and building took on a more sinister air, when the lights were turned off and the last of the doors were locked, the display lights were left on. The hissing of the furnaces now could clearly be heard through the hallways and floors.

February

The snow was piled high on the streets on the first Monday of the month and as always, the east elevator stopped at every one of the twelve floors on the way up to Belmont Furs, indicator light bulbs clicking along with every floor as its motor hummed a monotonous drone, the gold chained operator staring into the corner, timing for every brake. The elevator stops at twelve, the heavy brass doors open, Ivan steps out onto the hallway floor, the operator closes the door, sinks out of sight.

The baby was born a week ago. A boy. They named it Mikolai. Ivan could not bear to look at the boy or his wife, he could not even look at himself in the mirror anymore.

In the office looming over a cutting table Mr. Fielding was standing, smoking a fat Havana cigar. Sporting a bad comb-over and bad hygiene, he was married to a mail-order bride who begat him ungrateful children who would doubtless be after his small fortune when he died. That wouldn't be anytime soon, at fifty-two he was still able to bench press over eighty pounds at the gym.

Overweight in girth and ego he relished these immigrants, secretly taking pictures of lewd acts on his lunches and keeping them hidden. Ivan was his favourite, he got a hard on just thinking about the idiot. Gold chains and a tiny silver coke-spoon hang from his neck running down behind his two hundred-dollar silk shirt.

On this day, Ivan, dumping unused scraps in the B1 storage locker, dropped his cigarette lighter through a floor grate. Now on a mission he took the freight down one level, retrieved the lighter. He heard a noise. Curious, he discovered by use of the lighter a never-used door. With some difficulty he opened it, and his Bic lighter revealed an unlit slate stairwell that coiled downward. Maybe there was something of value down there. The stairwell coiled, then straightened, leading forward then down more. The steps were uneven and made as if for a man the height of eight or nine feet, they were that widely spaced out. Careful not to lose his footing, Ivan found his way to what he supposed was fifty feet or so underneath a street or the nearby building, he was not sure.

His feet were now on a dry dirt floor of an antiquated boiler room, the room about twenty feet by thirty in diameter. It was lit by an eerie red glow of undetermined origin. The walls were made of stone, the ceiling arched to a peak about fifteen feet in height. It had blackened, crumbling equipment, which looked like they belonged in a 16th century torture chamber or a museum. There was an iron maiden in one corner, a stretching rack and a furnace. That seemed more recent, like it was from the 19th century. The coal furnace suddenly ignited, emitting eerie heat and

a bit more light. His mind reeled, was he dreaming? As his eyes adjusted he saw iron implements hung on the walls, and more importantly a pile of fur pelt scraps, some of considerable size, stacked against one of the walls. There was a work table for making fur garments with rusted, useless knives. There was a great yellowed sink basin that looked as if it were from 1930.

He turned the taps. They were rusted but still worked. This was a room with a history.

He spotted something sticking out of the wall between two stones, to his delight he found a wad of current fifty-dollar bills. It was valid currency... he was holding a half year's wages in his hands! "Not enough to quit my job, it would not be enough to sustain me and my family for long," he thought to himself as he made his way clumsily back up the oversized stairs.

No, he would quit the job and find another job somewhere, somehow. He would tell Fielding at once! He went straight to up the office.

"So you want to quit? Ivan, my little cock sucking man from Warsaw." Fielding went over to his desk, pulled out a packet. "You will be my slave for as long as I want. You see what I have here?" He threw some pictures, obviously from a hidden camera in his office. Ivan's heart sank. Blackmail!

"Now let's take an early lunch." He closed and locked his office door. "I feel especially hungry," he added as he unzipped.

March

Ivan had been making fur hats and stoles. The furs were well preserved down in the mysterious rooms, there was a series of tomb-like rooms interconnected, a catacomb in the city that nobody knew about. He did not know how far they extended, was too scared to discover something truly terrible, but he knew they were vast. He guessed the reason it was never discovered was that simple reason that the ancient passages were so deep down under the living city.

Feldman had been using him as usual, and he was sitting on the money he had found. He would get enough selling the hats and pelts, there were only simple cutting tools down there, the office was tightly locked up and there were security cameras installed. He would save enough money up and his young family would just go far away where Feldman would never find them, or he could commit murder without getting caught. He had to decide.

In his workings he had fashioned a mask, a bear face mashed together, complete with snout and teeth. He deemed it the murder mask. It put him in the mood for his secret labours. It was often hot in that room, he often worked shirtless, wearing this mask. The air down there filled with spores and ancient dust effectively disquieted his thinking. In the glow of the oil lamp these sessions put him in the frame of mind to commit murder. This was what he had to do. And he would have to wear the mask.

April

His secret room for two months now aroused, excited and invigorated him. The fur scrap supply was seemingly inexhaustible; it was his habit to do this exciting thing as early as four or five in the morning. The guard didn't show up until seven, the cleaners and the workers didn't show until seven thirty. The building lobby and hallways had no cameras. He had this room all to himself. He smuggled knives and supplies downstairs during the day. Feldman was growing suspicious; he was noticing missing things from the office but said nothing.

May

On the first Wednesday of the month at four thirty in the morning, as usual Ivan was down in his lair where there was no season, no light. The building upstairs smelled of pelts and fur as the lobby, hallways and workstations, unlike the private offices, were not air conditioned. It was summer outside. Berated and abused every day, he didn't care; he tuned out at lunchtime even when Feldman was at his raunchiest worst. Ivan didn't care about anything but his workings underground. He even half-forgot about the found money let alone his family.

Kalena often complained that he had promised her furs and riches when they came to the new world. "I have to wear this thin cloth coat in winter and summer. The other women at the market have furs. Can you not get me a fur coat? Just ask for a raise or get another job!" she would say. She had no idea of what was going on. But in his catacombs, wearing the murder mask, he had found contentment. She soon thought there was another woman. He started berating her, they grew ever more distant.

By this time, he had grown to love the trophy displays of the lobby, his wife's nagging and criticisms. His boss' perversions, which were by now growing ever more bizarre, didn't faze him at all. Ivan was pulling into himself so much he could hardly feel heat or cold or taste food he ate, he was becoming tiny inside himself, like a human Russian nesting-doll.

Feldman was growing tired of Ivan. He sensed that Ivan was over the humiliations and had gone to all lengths to re-traumatize him. He tried everything, having his driver Lenny watch, participate and verbally berate him but now the fucker seemed immune to his cruel taunts and abuse. He knew he was stealing cutting tools and work equipment from the office. He also knew he was coming to the building in in the wee hours of the morning. He had hired another employee else he could master, humiliate and destroy. He had shown him around the floor already. "This will be your workplace, you will replace Ivan, and I expect you to learn all that he does." He chuckled to himself. Maybe he would send Ivan's wife some pictures as a goodbye gift. "I want you to know how everything is done, who we are."

The second Tuesday of this month Ivan felt somehow "different". The walls of the buildings seemed to be breathing as he walked the dark streets of four a.m. He carried the backpack up the sloping hill of the streets as was the usual. The stuffed animals of the lobby were alive that morning. The stoat, ermine and beaver were whispering to each other in secret. He could hear everything.

The breathing of the marble, the slate steps, echoed between his ears. In the room the stones seemed alive, to inhale and exhale; the dirt floors seemed to be soaking into his bare feet. Things were different today, he felt this was the day. He took off his shirt, pulled on the murder mask and wrapped the fur cloak around his neck. Now he was complete.

But this morning he had been spotted entering the building. Feldman had been watching from his limo parked just out of sight from the entrance as his driver Lenny calmly waited. He did a few more lines of coke in the back seat before entering the west side of the building. He would take the west elevators to the twelfth floor; the service elevator was too slow. But the light in the office wasn't on, the door was locked. "He must be in the storage." He rushed to the freight. The damn elevator was so slow. The elevator arrived, he knew how to operate the elevator. He patted his side; his revolver was ready. He was going to escort the hapless idiot to the police station and then send his pathetic wife those pictures.

He heard noise down below. Walking down the giant uneven stairs with some difficulty. "So this is where the stolen tools are." The noises were louder, grunting, red light ahead. "And what sick ritual is he practicing down here?" he thought as he approached.

And there he was, chanting. The words were unintelligible.

"Well, well, well... my little cocksucker is playing caveman," George said as Ivan turned, his eyes clearly visible through the irregular bear mask.

"So that's where the tools are." He pulled out his gun, aimed it at Ivan. He then took in the medieval torture devices and the piled-up pelts.

"So you've been stealing fur pieces too." This was perfect. But something was not right.

He pulled at his collar. "Why is it so hot in here?" A pause. "Say something, you idiot! Take off that headpiece!" There was movement in a corner. The red light of the furnace must be playing tricks. "What are these rooms? Answer me or I'll shoot you right now!"

Ivan stood his ground shoeless and fixed. Feldman began to feel fear.

"Say something!" He fired a warning shot on the dirt floor, lighting up the room with a flash. To the side of the standoff, an elaborate stitching of pelts swelled like a balloon. Creaking noises of bones splitting and forming could be heard. Feldman swung around and fired at the figure that was taking form, rising now to the height of ten feet. It had two arms and four legs, a patchwork grizzly with no eyes. The eyeless bear was on four legs yet stood upright. All six legs bore giant claws, two free arms at its side. Feldman fired again and again at the massive creature to no effect until he was out of bullets.

He threw the gun down in panic. It was coming at him. A massive free arm rose up into the air, claws splayed out. The length of a man, the effigy of life had no trouble with reach as Feldman's right arm was cleanly ripped from its socket. It landed on the dirt floor by a pile of skins. Again a swipe and Feldman's head flew off, bounced off the work table resting at Ivan's feet. The headless, one-armed Feldman fell to the ground. The gushing blood looked black in the red light as the dry dirt greedily sucked it up.

Ivan instantly grabbed Feldman's head and raised it to the creature who was now on all six legs and still easily the height of a man. Ivan burst out in laughter.

"At last at last I am truly free!" He carried the body and arm to the storage room and proceeded up the stairs with his trophy in hand.

Mr. Feldman had said to come in if he had not returned in a half hour. Lenny went in the west side entrance Feldman had entered, the door was unlocked. The lobby had always given him the creeps. Those mouldy dead animals.

There was someone on the other side. By the light of the display cases Lenny could see that the figure was wearing a fur coat or cloak, was hooded, barefoot and carrying what appeared to be a wax head. But there was liquid dripping from the neck. The figure went through the door leading behind the display cases.

As Lenny followed, his shiny black shoes slid, and he almost fell on the polished floor. He looked down and there were faint red footprints on the floor with a trail of drips that was blood. The head was real, and it now looked all too familiar in his memory. After a time, Lenny looked up and what he saw made him reel as the room spun.

He saw the decapitated heads; a woman and a baby and Mr. Feldman mounted on a birch stump with a tasteful painted blue sky background. Ivan had killed Kalena and little Mikolai in their sleep that morning before leaving the apartment. He had carefully positioned Feldman so he would be staring at his departed family as they gazed out at the glass.

Lenny was frozen; he could see his

own image as his mind tried to understand the macabre display. He could not move his eyes and did not hear the masked murderer approaching from behind. He did not feel the sharp blow to the neck as his neck vertebrae and nerve chord were instantly severed.

That morning the day guard discovered Lenny's headless body on the lobby floor, the bloodied fire axe and the four heads in the case. Also Ivan's body, slumped by the freight elevator staring into his own peculiar void, covered in blood, murder mask clenched in his hands. It was there on that floor that Ivan's heart just stopped working. This murdering baby-killer of a man, who towards the end of his tortured life was numbed to the world and had crawled in and out of himself, and in turn was driven to madness by forces unseen from a labyrinth of inverted sanity and reason.

June

The building's lobby was taped off for that week. The investigation led to the freight elevator and eventually the locker where Mr. Feldman's headless corpse was found (right arm detached, laid across his chest) in the B1-12 storage locker. It was soon discovered that a janitor key (from a little-used set), which allowed access into the building and main floor, was missing. Until the

gruesome murders this had gone unnoticed.

On the twelfth floor the sex photos were discovered by police but largely ignored and somehow "never existed" to protect the family name. The murders made for great copy. The four decapitated heads and bodies made the Allo-Police tabloid sell out at the newsstands. A lot of talk about cult and devil worship was made but nothing proven. The lobby display cases were demolished, the cavities in the lobby walls sealed up.

2015

The building houses several dressmakers, jewellers, an adult career college, and outside on La Rue Mayor the pricy patio bar Le Falco. The building now has centralised air conditioning. The catacombs and the creature are still undiscovered. The horrible events of that second Tuesday of May 1980 are largely forgotten.

THE END

ABOUT THE AUTHOR

Dean Wirth's influences include Lovecraft, Kafka, Poe and the classic Universal movies. His story 'Organic Life' was published in spring 2017 in 'Polar Borealis' and he has also been previously published in Lovecraftiana. Dean is married and lives in Alberta Canada with three dogs.

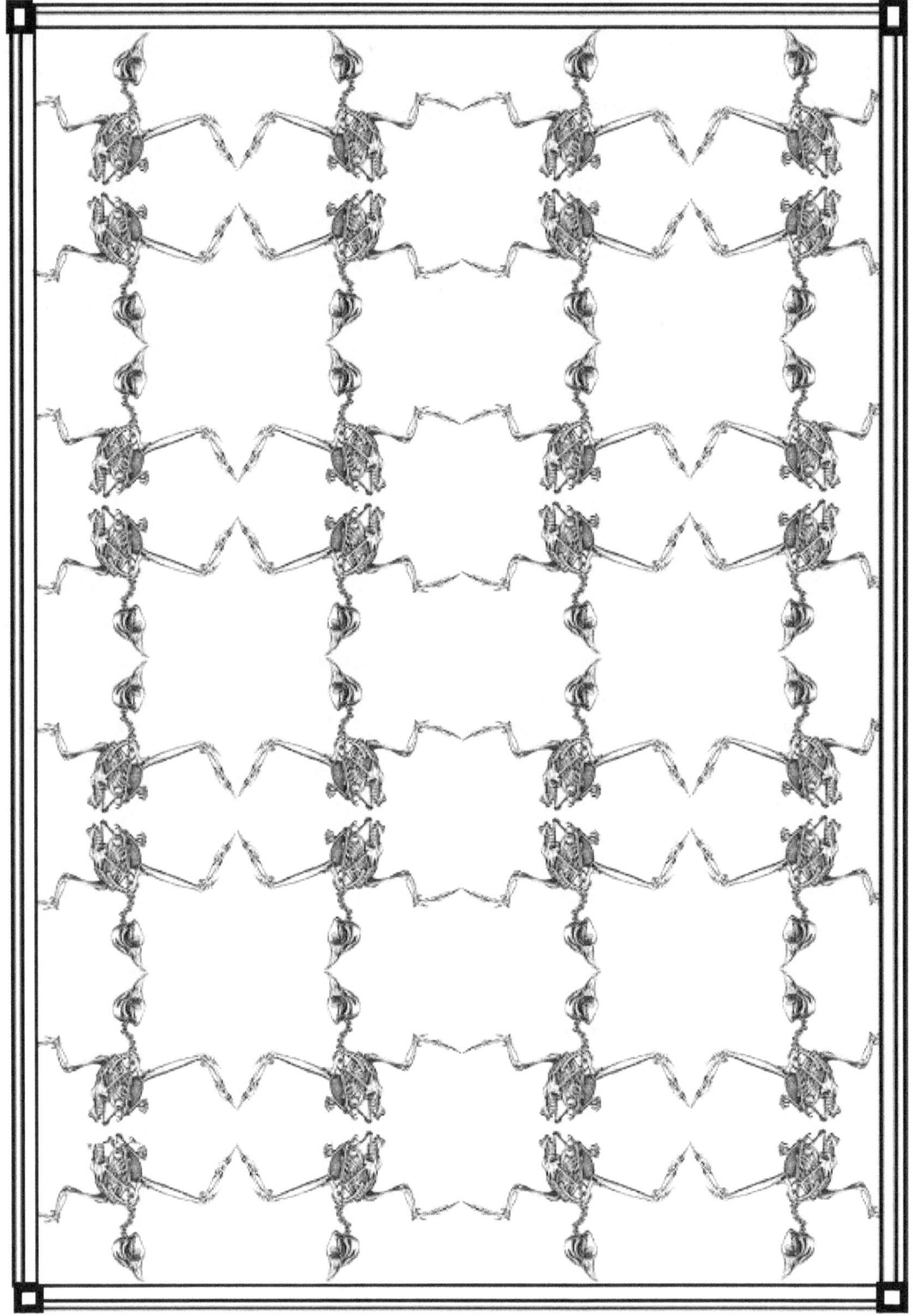

Dean Wirth

www.ingramcontent.com/pod-product-compliance
Lightning Source LLC
Chambersburg PA
CBHW081409180626
46811CB00017BA/3221